D0555530

SIDEBROW BOOKS

NONE OF THIS IS REAL

Published by Sidebrow Books
P.O. Box 170113
San Francisco, CA 94117-0113
sidebrow@sidebrow.net
www.sidebrow.net

Cover art by Monica Canilao
Cover & book design by Jason Snyder

ISBN: 0-9814975-4-3
ISBN-13: 978-0-9814975-4-9

FIRST EDITION | FIRST PRINTING
9 8 7 6 5 4 3 2 1
SIDEBROW BOOKS 005
PRINTED IN THE UNITED STATES

Sidebrow Books titles are distributed by
Small Press Distribution

Titles are available directly from Sidebrow at
www.sidebrow.net/books

A Member of
Inter
section
incubator
Services for Artists
www.theintersection.org

Sidebrow is a member of the Intersection Incubator, a program of
Intersection for the Arts (www.theintersection.org) providing fiscal
sponsorship, networking, and consulting for artists. Contributions
to Sidebrow are tax-deductible to the extent allowed by law.

NONE OF THIS IS REAL

MIRANDA MELLIS

SIDEBROW BOOKS • 2012 • SAN FRANCISCO

FACE

Here is what happened. I became ill suddenly. I tried to act normally, taking walks with friends, eating chocolates, giving advice. But then it would rise up in me. My face moving involuntarily, twitching, leering, telling a story over which I had no control. The illness subsided if I was by myself or only incidentally with strangers (on the bus, in line at the café, passing in the hallways of houses or buildings). But if there was a deeper acquaintance, some superstructure of expectation to companionship, a closeness or depth of feeling or sincerity required, the attack was triggered. The walks, the talks, the chocolates, the advice giving—it seemed they would destroy me.

We would walk right to the edge of high cliffs, a small crowd marveling at the vista. Beautiful? Opaque. Trying to find meaning in the view, my face would start its antic, sneering rebellions. I couldn't enjoy the view with the others. My body was rejecting meaning, or so it seemed. At the very least, I had learned to refrain from complaining, or even speech. In not speaking I became a plateau.

My cheerful companions tried to keep things light, understandably unnerved by my facial aggressions. Truly, a person may become an abyss: I felt it happening to me. My visage became a kaleidoscopic mask; people weren't sure who they were looking at. I could not translate. I felt nonexistence encroaching. Occasionally some little thing would bring happiness, a coy green halter, a wagging tree, a muscular baby, a black shadow like ink moving. Overall, however, I could see I was rapidly deteriorating. How frighteningly miniature my world had become: the size of a face. If I had ever been in a scene (and I had), those days were gone. I remained friends with two people whose faces hid nothing. With them, I took my ease and cleared my mind.

Otherwise, my body interpreted greetings as tests, glances as warnings, quotidian egotism as dangerous predation. It responded with terror to unspoken demands. It revolted especially against ceremonies of praise and recognition. It twitched crazily and changed every subject to the outright madness of my face. On the one hand, the ugliness of resentment, with nothing like progress to show; on the other, the masking of loss. And its concomitant—revenge. Exhausting revenge! I have a relative who disappeared and this caused irreparable damage to the immediate family, all of whom descended into various forms of addiction and personality disorder. Of course, the point was revenge; otherwise, she would have contrived to reappear.

Her future is fixed, a callus. My own is shrouded in mystery. Will it have been long and convulsive? Or brief, a mere exhalation? I do not know and so for what do I prepare?

NONE OF THIS IS REAL

The first night on a visit to see his mother, O hardly slept on an emaciated mattress in the trough of an old sofa bed. He had dreamt of a vast construction site made of thin, gray plastic rods that, like the intersecting leaves of the horsetail plant, were easily adjoined or separated. The site was porous, open to the elements. Here and there people "worked," which consisted of sticking the rods together and then pulling them apart. An angry foreman told O in despair that he was the only one who knew the truth: the whole work site was a façade. His job was to hide the truth from the workers, forever. O remarked to the foreman that the workers might notice for themselves, as pulling the rods apart and then sticking them back together was self-evidently meaningless. The foreman shook his head. You don't understand, he said; they wouldn't know unless I told them and I'm hired not to. Is your work pointless too then? O asked. No, said the foreman; I keep everything going. What would happen if you told them? O asked. I would lose my job, the foreman replied sadly, turning away.

In the morning O's mother Sonia had come upon him standing in a curious way with his head turned all the way to the left and tilted slightly forward. O had always been a quiet person, which his mother appreciated, but this visit he seemed to talk less than ever. What Sonia had once found a comforting quietude in her son now registered as a nameless despair. She hadn't seen him in a year, and now this, an unexpected visit that found him drooping by the foldout.

Sonia asked how O slept. He had insomnia, he said, though whale songs sometimes lulled him to sleep. Sonia found the whale songs disturbing. If they helped him sleep, they kept her awake. Their melancholy cries, like accusing ghosts, made her restless, left her up late working on her piecemeals.

Sonia offered him breakfast. O came into the kitchen and sat down. She poured coffee. Gradually O became unusually animated and talkative. He couldn't recall when he had last felt so vivid. He inquired after the Blackwater training site recently completed outside of her town. She didn't know what he was talking about. Freelance mercenaries, he said. She didn't know anything about that, she said; she thought they had built a new mall. He'd read that malls were constructed such that they could easily be converted into internment camps; did she know about that? That sounds like conspiracy theory to me, she said, pouring him a second cup, to which he rejoined, more like conspiracy practice.

The coffee tastes different, he said suddenly. She shrugged. I've switched to regular, she said; maybe that's it. But you don't drink regular, O said. I drink regular, she said; it gives me a lift. Why didn't you tell me you switched? O asked, standing up. He walked out of the kitchen. Sonia followed and asked, What difference does it make? But what was he doing?

He stood in the hallway in that discomfiting way, his spine cambered. He gazed sideways at a photograph of his grandmother Aletria as he furled and swayed like a water lily in an invisible current.

If they wanted to round everyone up, he resumed suddenly, they could sweep the malls on Black Friday. Malls are radial, he exclaimed, easily convertible to panopticons. The police could stand in the core of the mall and they could see everything, keep everyone in view and at a distance at the same time, by clearing out the merchandise. Once the dream catchers, hood ornaments, shredders, tarps, plastic ivy, glue traps, proverbs, bibelots, electric fences, candelabras, sonar kits, ottomans, dog beds, bait, potpourris, pillows, varnish, and incense are removed from the shelves the police will be able to see clear through the mall across walkways, windows, and escalators right through all that shatter-proof glass, ever-lit, and pen the consumers in their troughs.

An on-and-off unit-producer of impulse buys, Sonia shook her head disapprovingly. They're not going to round up consumers, she said, or commodity artisans. You mean factory workers, he said. They're not going to round up consumers, she repeated. Speaking of pillows, she said suddenly, I have a present for you! She brought out a small, embroidered pillow decorated with a cartwheeling jester and a banner that read, *Life's Too Mysterious Don't Take It Serious!* O straightened up, held the pillow in his hands and stared. It takes thousands of pounds of fuel to visit you by plane, he said. I made it myself, she replied. He placed the pillow on a chair and leaned back over to sway, folded into an abrupt silence. I made the pillow, Sonia repeated. Thank you, O said. You're welcome, she said; pillows are easy—they have four sides and one side opens, like a room. Like a stanza, O replied.

Why are you standing like that? Sonia asked. This is my position, he said. What is? Sonia asked. Get into my position, he replied. Sonia put her hand out in front of her. No, I don't get it, she said.

My therapist taught me how to find my position, he explained. Staring at the floor, swinging as he listed, O proceeded to tell his mother about his therapy. He hadn't planned on telling her. But once he started, he couldn't stop.

To begin with my therapist herself had difficulty finding her position, O said, a position she could sustain in comfort. It took her a long time but it was worth the search, or so she said, although the position she found allowed her to continue only with a few special clients, O went on, because it consisted of her lying on the floor with her knees up by her chest, which was off-putting for some people. For others, such as myself, O said, the sight of her on the floor with her knees up on her chest was encouraging. Sonia strained to comprehend. Tiara Scuro provides something permanent, O explained, a personal position to which we can always return. You should try it, he said.

Not long after they met, O's therapist, Tiara Scuro, narrated for O the inspiration for her technique. He had just finished cleaning her office when she came in unexpectedly, a bottle of wine in hand, offering him a drink. She poured and explained that her business had failed. But that turned out to be a blessing in disguise, she told O. For years I had been removing the ground from underneath my clients, she said. But then I realized that what people really want is exactly what I was trying to subtract: a position, a Patch of Stability, a bit of personal ground in a time when *actual* ground is inaccessible for a variety of economic and environmental reasons, and in a time when positions, in the sense of steady employment, are scarce. So now I offer customized stability through what I call Path to a Position.™

She outlined for O the steps by which he would, with her, find his position. She encouraged him to abandon his political despair, his doubts and misgivings. The old school believed the antidote for despair was courage, she said, but the real anti to the dote is a comforting distortion; this is what I call somatic realism.

It was that day, O remembered, that he'd suddenly noticed how elegant Tiara's stiff gray dress was, the way it stood at attention around her, her sash like a soft saber.

We became involved, O told his mother, and she often joked about marriage. She called it the universal cult. She brought it up so often that I thought she was hinting. So I proposed.

What happened? Sonia asked after a few moments of silence. When I proposed, O went on thinly, she withdrew into her position on the floor with her knees up to her chest. And I withdrew into mine as well, as she had taught me to do, leaning as you now see me, and she said, Let us be married only to our positions.

Sonia's mind wandered, ghosting in and out. After a mutually obscure pause, she declared she'd best clean up after breakfast. O swayed, recollecting the last thing Scuro had said before she broke off contact: I don't want to spend the rest of my life praising you. I prefer positions to declarations.

— ∞ O ∞ —

As a child O had halfheartedly tried to fulfill his mother's fantasies of him being a great student. But he much preferred his own fantasy of becoming a great author. He wished to write a novel instead of doing homework. He intended to write an encyclopedic, world-historical novel and to let it speak for him, with all the formal eloquence of a book. A book has symmetry, proportion, whereas he was asymmetrical, all out of proportion. And so he tried to write it, in pencil. He wrote it instead of doing schoolwork, in bed over time, where he lay with headaches and backaches, side aches and everything aches. Even thought ached like a chafed little snake.

When it was complete he placed his manuscript into the hands of his favorite teacher, Mrs. Lee. Although a child then, O had felt older than Mrs.

Lee. For she was beautiful enough to take attention for granted, whereas he was world-weary enough to be grateful for it. O told her that if he had possessed her beauty, he would not have been a teacher. She asked him what he would have done instead. He would become an airhead, he said, or maybe a trophy wife. He would not suffer children nor bother to write a book, let alone learn history or try to make sense of it. There would be no need to make sense of things. When one was beautiful one was sense itself. Mrs. Lee wondered where O had picked up the expression "trophy wife." From a game show, he said, called *Who Wants to Remain Infantile?*

Mrs. Lee read O's manuscript with care. But her responses were dis-illusioning for him. There was a conference with his mother Sonia about O's mental health. He had had no answers to her red-inked questions: *Why is there only one person in the chorus? What happened to the organ meat gun? It goes off, and then we never see it again. Do the dogs have actual human hands or are they prosthetic? What about the fish? Whose body parts are we supposed to take seriously? Most of all, where are the humans? How can we care if there are no humans?* But he didn't know. He just wrote; he didn't analyze. Years later, when he moved out of his mother's apartment and was sorting his boxes, O found the manuscript. He was humiliated all over again. In a prolonged, physically demanding and self-castigating gesture of ritual disavowal, he burnt his first literary attempt in an empty parking garage behind the Big Lot, down the street from where he and Sonia lived with their unpredictable old dog, Violet Ray. The moment the old pages had turned entirely to ash his shame turned into regret.

Sonia spent a lot of time alone. Violet Ray the dog had kept Sonia com-pany while she performed stay-at-home or temporary jobs ranging from home-manufacturing mail-order dolls and crochet fruit to participating in medical experiments, which, although they sometimes had adverse emotional and physical effects, were remunerative enough. She once saw a poster geared toward discouraging students from participating in such trials. It showed a young white man in a hospital gown on a cot. *You went to school to study*, it admonished, *not to become one*. The message was not addressed to her. She was not expected to learn but to labor. She resignedly donated her mechanical capacities to production and her autonomic activities to science. She regretted having participated in one when O was in utero. She secretly worried that his difficulties stemmed from that drug trial. I *hate* school, he'd suddenly burst out as a child. But you're so smart, she urged. She tried to explain that college would be different. There his intelligence would be appreciated. His looks would not count. He didn't believe her. Look at you, he said, a lot of good schooling has done you. Yes, she chose to reply sincerely, a lot of good.

— ∞ O ∞ —

When O had first conceived the idea of relocating, his only reference was the town his grandmother Aletria had lived and died in, three states away. He decided to move there. He found a cheap apartment. He took a part-time job as a page at a library. He called his mother more often than either of them would have predicted. He continued to aspire to write an unprecedented, encyclopedic, world-historical novel. But it was increasingly apparent — though he tried to ignore this oppressive knowledge — that new techniques in climate change adaptations, urban agriculture, toxic waste mitigation, soil remediation, foreclosure opportunism, oil spill cleanup, sex, self-defense, clairvoyance, and air and water filtration were considered more pressing than literary innovation. Climate change in particular gave him nightmares. The only answer he could think of was to re-evolve, or devolve, archaic equipment to tolerate heat and breathe underwater.

Thick skins, gills, and fins. Animal adaptation seemed more promising than human politics anyway, though natural selection was known for taking its time. Rather than trying to fix the environment, he wondered if genetic engineers shouldn't focus on turning humans back into fish. Or perhaps forward into machines? He wrote a letter proposing his ideas. He didn't know where to send it. He addressed it To Whom It May Concern. Occasionally he would dream about these things. He dreamt of breathing underwater, his skin thick and smooth as a dolphin's. Or he could see in the dark, his eyes secreting light.

When he later learned that mass extinctions from the greenhouse effect would not include his species, which had brought it about, he was even more horrified by the injustice of cause and effect.

He barely earned a living at the library, but he bided his time and tried to outline his book. The outlines were always eroding and changing, like seashores or minds. Money came in small amounts and denominations. Bills were like a seasonal predator for him. Regularly the total absence of money threatened to do him in. He was grateful for the library job because it kept the predator outside the gates. He also imagined that the constant proximity to books would be a prod. He'd glean something new every day for what he called his "unbearable correspondences" file. For instance each of the 6 billion people on Earth used an average of 3.5 pounds of wood daily, which came to nearly 4 billion tons per year. But he never used wood. He understood, however, that he would always be implicated within the mathematical category of the "average" no matter what he did or refrained from doing. He read that in France, during the Reign of Terror, the executioner would show the just-decapitated head its own body so that, in its last seconds, consciousness was forced to comprehend itself irreversibly cleaved. The anonymity of the executioner was maintained so that everyone would be implicated as consenting perpetrators of capital punishment, for if nothing else, one always belonged to the state. By the time the monstrous share reached the individual, however, it hardly bore weight at all. In fact, for some, the state weighed less than a feather, while others it crushed. O knew, however, that no matter whether he himself disagreed with capital punishment or never used wood, he was complicit in both executions and the destruction of habitats. This knowledge was important to his novel, he intuited, though he wasn't sure how.

Unfortunately, being surrounded by pages had not so far made him produce very many. Furthermore, his job as a page required that he continuously touch, asymptotically peruse, and numerically vet printed matter. Naturally, on his days off, he was given to contemplating his yawning reflection in a convex spoon (the distortions of which, he felt, improved his appearance).

O collected several folders' worth of materials he considered relevant towards the novel he intended to write, which he conceived of as a post-political social-realist novel (he found no contradiction in the terms), a transnational, literary, neoteric, polyphonic *Salt of the Earth*, or a revamped, reflexive, more rounded *Life in the Iron Mills*, complicatedly dramatizing individual stories behind global struggles to reclaim life's basic necessities which, down to genetic material, were being increasingly privatized. He wore his Yoda shirt to work. "Do or do not. There is no try." Pop rhetoric and ancient ideas were processed and denatured by industries just like any other raw material. But if mining, refining, and manufacturing were the doom of living things, at least decontextualized slogans and faces grafted ornamentally onto commodities weren't in and of themselves linked to cancer.

O's files, strictly contemporaneous, included occasional bright episodes such as articles that described farmers resisting corporate seed and plant gene patents. Or homemade oyster mushroom and hair mats, invented by a barber to absorb oil roiling up on various shores and tangled riverbanks, where locals defied "security details"—guarding catastrophes like property—to fight for the right to clean up industrial waste. But such reports appeared to be far outnumbered by repetitive clips on domestic abuse, fratricide, matricide, patricide, gendercide, island massacres, city bombings, school shootings, gang wars, piracy, and other forms of local and daily violence on land and at sea—quotidian wars in miniature, mimicking the psychoses of militarized globalism, dominating, self-righteous, exclusionary, and retaliatory. If only people relied on physical positions, O thought as he read, instead of ideological ones.

His "unbearable correspondences" dossier allowed O to emotionally modulate his experience. He imagined the perpetrators and victims in the stories he read with their heads hooded, their individuality filed away. He did this in order to study the average of power and its exercises.

He would read until headaches made it impossible or until his eyes burned and he felt a sizzle behind his sternum, the sound of his heart's little fire going out. His dossier was called Apocalypse Forever. Compiling a file wasn't difficult. Organization came naturally. As a child he had loved to play office, preferring stapling to scissoring, arranging to ripping, gluing to wrecking, and folding to shooting.

His files were always in order. However, he became depressed and skeptical when it came time to use them—in short, when it came time to write. He was paralyzed by the messy, sorrowful wilderness of all that content and he could not get over the feeling that the documents spoke best for themselves, like geological strata, or the ephemera under glass at his library; they only asked to be interpreted and studied. How could he improve upon storied truth? The problem was a grass trap every which way he turned: what was the good of imagining reality? And if there was no such thing as time or progress, why keep recapitulating those falsehoods in the form of chronologies? He had learned that women could legally own property and practice surgery thousands of years ago, while as recently as a hundred they could do neither. The moderns were surely older than the ancients. Knowledge came and went like the tides. Diachronic history was chronic; retrospection moved forward; information zigzagged like a dying cowboy. Time itself moved like water. Factual records looked like frightening art when the tide went out on patriarchy, God, and war. You worry too much, his mother would say; your worries enclose my worries, like a fence around a fence.

Instead of writing, O would file, re-categorize materials, or, if his head hurt particularly badly, shop for pillows. He had developed a chronic sore neck. His cranium felt heavier. His neck was unequal to it. How the head pounded, with a lacerating pain right between the brains. And lately there were allergies, to what he did not know. As they were worse in the mornings, he suspected they were to his mattress or his old, flat pillow. Obsessively but unproductively he researched bedding. He looked at down pillows, hypoallergenic pillows, hemp pillows, and those very long, tubular, surrogate-lover pillows. They were all so expensive. He never purchased one. He rebuked time wasted on dreaming of pillows, as if pillows and time were to blame.

He went to work early and stayed late. He wandered among thousands of books spread out over floor after fluorescent floor, opening them at random.

What was he looking for? he asked himself. A brochure on the floor for Tiara Scuro's Path to a Position™ caught his eye. It showed ordinary people in ordinary clothes contorted variously, mouths open and eyes closed, sculptures at a silent party. He was drawn to this undemanding-looking social setting.

He called to inquire but the fees took his breath away. He shyly tried to hang up but the voice on the other end of the line lowered her price precipitously though it was still too high. O apologized for his lack of finances and Scuro proposed barter. In exchange for cleaning her office, she would give him a series of sessions.

O scrubbed Tiara Scuro's floors and walls with vinegar, as was her wish. Her office, largely empty with high windows and smooth floors, had a peculiar effect on O when alone in it late at night. He would get on the floor and slide around on his side. He pressed his cheek against the window. He raced in circles around the perimeters of the room in a rolling chair, blowing. He opened his mouth wide and lunged at his own reflection.

In their first session O told Tiara about how Sonia didn't return his calls. Sometimes he called his mother many times in a row, a rising desperation in his chest. If you were an animal in those moments, Scuro asked, what would you be doing? O thought he'd be a bug on his back trying to turn over. From this image they constructed the first of his several positions, "helpless insect," in which he enacted his inability to affect his mother, waving his limbs in the air, no one to turn him over. Later he found his favorite position, "silk cravat in a river," which proved erotic to Scuro. When she spontaneously embraced him, O was so confused that at first he thought she was having a seizure. When she kissed him he wondered if he had lost his mind. It was as though he had had a letter to deliver, and had been on a mile-long line at the post office that had been moving one inch a year. Existence was waiting on that line. If expecting to get to the counter and buy a postage stamp and an envelope had seemed reasonable enough at the start, over the years he had simply forgotten that there was a counter, or even what he might require if he arrived there—he just waited without knowing why. Now he was suddenly catapulted to the head of line and was being handed a book of glossy, fruity stamps, which he licked eagerly. His message was finally enveloped and sent.

When the relationship ended as abruptly—if not as surprisingly—as it began, he was quietly hysterical. The sudden loss of unhoped-for love kept him awake at night. He tried to talk to his mother about it but she was unresponsive. He lurked self-consciously around the self-help section of the library, even when he wasn't working. It was a genre he had never noticed until now. The first time he had approached the section, he was astonished by the brightly colored titles blaring words like SHAME and ANGER across the stacks.

Occult, illness, dying, sex, and relationships were among the larger sub-categories, while the flagship, self-help, consisted of innumerable books with sentence-long titles. One night he found it in disarray, as though someone had had a paroxysm in the sex and relationships sections, books desperately strewn on the floor, messy piles staggered around a small wooden stool, big gaps in the shelves. A young woman O had not met yet, another page with thick long black hair paved flat and glistening, was restoring order to the section. She reshelved books and pushed protruding titles back into place with the radiant calm of the beatified.

When she had gone, O pulled out a small pile of self-help books and sat at the end of the section. He leafed around. The books were repetitive. Especially prevalent was the argument that reality was a product of individual will.

He scanned shelves and pages and made note of the proliferation of self-hyphenations: self-destruction, self-actualization, self-improvement, self-promotion. It seemed the self was a problem that required a variety of ministrations. Self-exposure appeared to be the panacea. Who could pull it off? A fin of doubt cut around his skull. He had the idea that he was on the outside of something good, trawling its perimeters, prevented by an immutable unknown from penetrating a foggy exterior membrane towards … what? A vivid interior? He had a memory of going to his grandmother's house and he thought her vagina was like a motel. His mother's was much homier. Then he thought, Vagina? That was not the word he was looking for. He meant house.

The page with paved black hair returned. O thought he detected the scent of a freshly mown lawn. Their eyes locked for a moment. She smiled carefully, her teeth shone behind her lips, soft glossy slopes he might never traverse. His face felt enormous. He looked around for shelter, resisting the temptation to get into his position in public. The human back is a protective barrier, O thought. He quietly rotated towards the corner until his face, all seven orifices, was out of view. Turned thus, his back like a closed gate, O decided to give his full attention to this heretofore-unconsidered genre, one that combined the manual with the parable. These were myths and fairy tales stripped down to parts. The numbered charts, series of questions, steps, diagrams, and other procedures resembled detritus at a narrative construction site, the materials and methods aspiring authors of fiction were also taught to use—ways of fleshing. In other words, self-help borrowed the techniques of the novel.

He examined the author photos. The writers smiled with white teeth. Their faces looked at you as from the happiest of days. These technicians of happiness advised reliving scenes of childhood in order to revise those scenes to suit. Another strategy was to make of the present a tabula rasa upon which any image whatsoever might be superimposed. They expressed their ideas in pithy mottos, such as "never do a man's laundry because men respect bitches," "you deserve a car," "you deserve the love you want," "you deserve to live forever." Deservingness was a theme, but on what basis did anyone deserve these things? O wondered. How were cars, romance, or immortality "rights"? Who would be the first immortal? Did everyone secretly think, "Me; I'll be chosen." By what criteria? Simply avowing God-given prerogatives—like tyrants and colonialists? He loitered over one book on the use of affirmations. The book asked what were his negative beliefs? And advised him to recite them in reverse. I am ugly and poor, O thought. Then he reversed it: I am not ugly; I am not poor. Was he doing it right? There were easily fifteen or more books on the subject of affirmations alone. What was the logic here? He tried again: I am not filled with doubt.

There was so much self-help to be doing, so many life-altering word games to play that O became fatigued. He leafed halfheartedly through one last book, *Stand-in for a Proxy*. He read a line in the book. "Life is a movie and you are the director." His mother would have agreed that life was a movie, but not that she was the director. For Sonia life was above all a place imagined by someone else, in which you were forced to live. One had no say in the matter. When he was a child, she would wave her arms around and declare, *None of this is real!* She'd hum her favorite tune, *Row, row, row your boat, life is but a dream*. Her platitudes maddened him. He'd purposefully forgotten the pillow she'd made him the last time he visited. But she ran down the street after him, flourishing it absurdly. He'd had no room in his luggage and had to carry it on the plane. It sat on his lap. His seatmate read it over O's shoulder. My mother made it, O explained. Lucky you, she said with a bitter little eye. Tired of life, yet she coveted the pillow; when's the last time she got a gift?

He studied the pillow's motto. Life was indeed mysterious, but that didn't make it unreal. Didn't the fact that life was too mysterious mean precisely that one should take it seriously? Yes, life was a serious mystery; it was not an unserious one. He preferred *serious* to *mysterious*. *Mystery* was disappointingly incoherent TV specials on the paranormal that Sonia liked to watch. Always the same "puzzling evidence," cow mutilations and such. Where there's smoke there's fire, she would say, an unrealist. If the horseshit starts piling up, there's a pony in the vicinity; maybe we're all aliens, who knows? Somebody knows, O protested mentally to the inner Sonia. But his imaginary mother listened no better than the enfleshed one.

O heard a quick step and recalled himself to his surroundings. He had been leafing through *Surrogates for Alternates* when a courier brushed by giving him an electric thrill. O watched him jog away. The man had a Hermes logo on his uniform. You could not help but think of Achilles when you thought of Hermes, O thought, Achilles with his fatal flaw in the very location of Hermes' tiny foot-wings. Body parts had specific kinds of meaning. In the system of astrology he had learned that each body part was a metonym for a sign's power. But weren't astrological signs themselves metonyms? Where did metonymy end? Did the body as a whole represent anything? What was its message? Like Hermes, life had a message. It was fleet, or fleeting, or perhaps fleeing on a fragile track. If you couldn't wing it, the track shattered under your weight. You had to have strong joints. The knee joint was associated with Capricorn ambitiously climbing the ladder of domination. From O's point of view, however, goats were not ambitious, but rather introspective. They climbed off to be alone, not to dominate. Nonetheless according to astrology, the goat, with its snake eyes and stiff hair, was considered power-hungry. Nixon and Mao were the usual exemplars.

Weary of self-improvement, O wandered through the stacks. He read around in a book called *The Scientific Revolution*. The sentence he landed on pinpointed his basic conundrum: *Method, broadly construed, is the preferred remedy for problems of intellectual disorder, but which method is it to be?* He read on and found what seemed at first an answer but in fact only intensified the problem. It was as if O himself was composed of the very corpuscles of the methodological dispute between early scientists. The "solution" ("it depends") made O feel scared, tired, and lazy all at once. You could not make an affirmation out of "it depends." Something was already decided.

O skimmed the introduction to what was reputed to be the first auto-biography, dictated by an illiterate thirteenth century mystic who had, like a self-helper, revised her life to suit her desire to marry Jesus: she had herself re-virginized. He opened another book a few shelves down. The Christian regime of excessively detailed sexual confession first took hold during the seventeenth century, it said. We sought thereafter to transform every desire into discourse. Memoir was an extension of the eight-centuries-long practice of confession, taking from that tradition the convention of detailing one's transgressions only in a book, or inside a booth, like a toy-theater, a stall, or a television studio. For the talk-show format it was helpful to have been utterly isolated in a long brutal night of trauma like Kasper Hauser and then suddenly burst onto the scene ahistorical and mostly naked like Britney Spears, ignoring linkages between child abuse and world wars. Hitler himself, O knew, had often been locked in a basement as a child. Just as European brutality towards people in the "New World" was as ordinary as torture and murder were quotidian at home, where inquisitors burned left-handed herbalists and their cats, so too, perhaps, had the famously abusive domestic lives of German families banalized violence for them, conditioned them to it. They treated their own children like broken objects, O thought; what stretch strangers?

War continued, moving from place to place, from kitchens and streets to deserts and oceans. You could see it all on TV, but what after all could be learned from war except war? All this exhibition and exposure had a paradoxically obscuring effect. One searched and searched. What was most dreaded was the absence of electricity. *I am not filled with doubt.* O wandered over to literary criticism. There he read that the author was dead. He did not want to hear that, as he had hoped to become one. He left, reciting, *I am not ugly. The author is alive.*

— ∞ O ∞ —

Headache after headache. What else to call the tormenting sensation of a forced point? Like the peak of a broken crown, the cephalalgy stabbed upward from the center of his ... mind? Brain? He felt the mysterious hurt bore him a message. But he was not photophobic or phonophobic. He did not have auras or nauseas. The pain was easily localized, but not easily remediated.

He tried sleeping with the pillow Sonia had made him. He woke up in the middle of the night drenched in sweat. The pillow smelled of Sonia— pharmaceuticals, mold, smoke, and sachets. He heard his downstairs neighbor, Crescent, moving around in her apartment, also sleepless apparently. She was a fortune-teller, a lover of the fickle moon in its guises, especially its sickle form when it was nascent, or conversely dying away. Outside her door hung a sign, *Cartomancy With Handmade Lunar Deck by Crescent Moon.* She wore cateye glasses, the kind worn by schoolteachers to frighten their pupils. She was one of those young ladies whose fashion is an homage to old ladies. Her own grandmother had never needed to change her feline look. Much of Crescent's various cat-themed accoutrements were acquired from her. O had seen them together walking down the street, like two memories of one lifetime.

It was just like them to be similar. Confused images merged in O's mind of the two Crescents, young and old, lightly treading an earthen road arm in arm; Sonia and Aletria quarreling; the messenger wearing the Hermes patch; the metallic taste of Tiara Scuro; shelf after shelf piled high to the sky with books; the sludgy sincerity of his mind. Suddenly the sound of Crescent singing and playing a guitar broke his reverie. He could hear every word:

The world's oldest leather shoe, a woman's size 7 lace-up
Was discovered in a cave, cold as a refrigerator, between Iran and Armenia,
Along with wine-making apparatus, and three human heads preserved
In jars
Radiocarbon dating
Confirms the shoe is from the Copper Age, when metal tools first appeared
5,600 years ago
It's 1,000 years older than the pyramids
400 years older than Stonehenge
Though even older footwear was found—a sandal 6,900 years old
In Missouri

She played the song continuously, altering the tune. By the third time she'd sung it through, O was penetrated with longing. How had he failed to notice there was a singing clairvoyant archaeology enthusiast right downstairs? It seemed like an omen. He poked his head out of his door, wrote down the number on her sign, and called to make an appointment.

— ∞ O ∞ —

The reading took place in the front room of Crescent's two-room studio, which had the same layout as O's but was sparser. There was a single bed, neatly made, a hot plate, a small refrigerator, and in the corner by a large, open picture window, a black rocking chair and her instrument on a stand. Above the chair hung a print of a Magritte painting, *Collective Invention*, in which a woman with a fish's head lies on the shore of the sea. Crescent unfolded the legs of a black card table that had been leaning against the wall across from the large picture window, with a view to a hundred tarmac rooftops, a world of pigeons, seagulls, roofers, lookers, and smokers. She snapped each leg into place. She spread the legs of two matching folding chairs, and she and O sat facing each other. Mounted on the walls were many tiny chairs of various materials—cans, walnuts, cane, porcelain; spirit chairs, she called them.

When Crescent asked him why he had come to see her, his throat closed and his chest ached. With difficulty he told her about his headaches and his book. He thought of saying something about her singing, but he did not. Crescent's face was neutral as she listened. She shuffled the cards in a matter-of-fact way, handed him the deck and politely requested that he cut it three times. She laid out ten cards face down in a spiral across the rickety card table.

Not feeling well, she said, book aches, headaches; what does pain want? What are the meanings? She turned over the cards. The first three cards were so-so-moon, so-like-the-moon, and moon-fool. Next she pulled shy-moon, moon-wolverine, moon-o-logue, moon-daycare-center, moon-milk, moon-pie, and shark-moon. She shuffled and pulled one more card: moon-corpse. O suddenly became aware of an antler lamp, swaying above, its thick black electrical cord emerging from behind Crescent, bisecting her head. Crescent studied the cards and then spoke at length; O tried to follow. He caught some of it ... *scorn mask ... cornhusks ... incorporeal ... bundles on fire ... corpus ... burning pages ... frozen sea ... O mega ... reincarnation ... train station ...*

Her interpretations eluded O's grasp. She may as well have been talking to a bird, he thought. What's a hierophant? he asked. A teacher figure, she said. The cards are saying that you have been burned by a teacher, is that true? But O's mind was blank. Doesn't ring a bell, he said. Crescent shuffled the deck once more, cut it, and laid down shark-moon and moon-corpse. Shark-moon depicted a shark shadow swimming through a moonlit ocean of corn. Moon-corpse depicted a skeleton rider thrown high from a bucking bull at a night rodeo. He was startled: moon-corpse again? Crescent frowned. She shuffled the deck three more times and turned over a last card: moon-corpse for the third time. O was frightened.

He stood up to leave. Hold on, she said, as she scribbled in a notepad, I have referrals for you. She tore out the page and handed it to him with a look of concern. He glanced at it unseeing, thanked her and left. In the hallway O saw a dusty print he hadn't noticed before, of a yellow bird with one canny eye dressed in circus garb, *Le Jongleur*. As he looked into the eye of the bird, he felt lonely. He had to admit, it seemed he had a disorder of some kind. And yet, he considered, everyone he had ever known had one, be it attention-deficit disorder, bipolar disorder, obsessive-compulsive disorder, post-traumatic stress disorder. Sometimes even disorders seemed to exhibit signs of order, coming in waves. O knew all complex systems to be inherently disorderly. Sonia had had bunions, shingles, amnesia, *and* depression.

When O got home he looked at the notepaper. Crescent had written down three names and phone numbers. The first was for a free clinic; the second was for a doctor who charged on a sliding scale; the third was for Crescent's teacher Skye, a past and future life reader.

O called the free clinic and left a message. The following week they called back and he was given a number to call in order to make an appointment to make an appointment. Eventually he made an appointment to make an appointment, but his appointment to make an appointment was months away. He had hoped to see someone sooner. He ended by calling the doctor Crescent had recommended in her note. The doctor herself answered immediately and said she could see him right away.

— ∞ O ∞ —

It seemed to O that the doctor's office concealed something. Paradoxically so, as the devices, implements, and charts all had but one purpose, which was to expose—but without revealing. He whistled into mindless space as he waited. Whatever is told to me in this room about the future of my body, he thought, can I believe it?

The doctor came in and examined him, rotating O slowly on a spinning chair. Did you wear tight caps as a child? she asked. No, he said, but I did wear a headgear. Aha! she exclaimed. Why did you have a headgear? Because I had fangs, he responded. Ah! But you still have fangs, she said. Yes, he replied simply. I had four fangs. She peered into his mouth. She palpated his skull. You need to get an MRI, she said. O's heart exfoliated. It pounded in his ears like an oil rig. His hands and feet were encased in ice. I don't have insurance, he said. In that case I'll do a telepathic MRI, she said. She handed him a laminated article she had written, faded and yellowed, and left the room telling him she'd be right back. He tried to read the article, but it was written in another language. Maybe static, he thought, which he could not decipher. The words looked like stunned mice to him, sliding around in snow.

When she returned a half hour later, the doctor told O that his brain had mutated, or torn. She held up a piece of paper. On it was a detailed line drawing, a representation of his brain with a leaf shape curving out of the hippocampus. You have developed a growth, she said. O thought it looked like a kite or a feather. No, the doctor replied, it's nothing like a kite or a feather. It's rigid, cartilaginous, more like a fin. He was faint. He should get a second opinion, came the thought, blowing by like a plastic bag. He suppressed a secondary despair: from whom would he get another opinion? He gingerly touched the top of his skull. There *was* something protruding under his hair, a little cone.

Ignoring him, the doctor got out her pendulum. Was he born with the errant flap or not? Where did it come from? Was it an organism, a mutation? The pendulum reading was indeterminate. O held the laminated page in both hands. The doctor paced. She opened a drawer and took out a bag of runes. She shook it and pulled out a little white stone. *Gateway*, she thought. She was at a threshold? She realized suddenly that the small pyramid was something very unusual. She abruptly left the room again to consult her library.

O stared at her laminated article written in static but he still couldn't make it out. Feeling vaporous he looked around the room. There were a series of prints the doctor must have torn out of an old calendar. Robert Mapplethorpe (July), Kandinsky (April), Georgia O'Keeffe (January). When the doctor returned, O was standing in front of Rothko (October). I've discovered a new form of cross-species parasitism, she exclaimed, a "jumping species"; this may be an evolutionary—or metaphysical, if you like—response to extinctions. O was rigid, hardly hearing, caught up in the word *discovered*. *Discovery*—he had learned in his auto-didactic pursuits—often connoted an exploitative enterprise: the discovery of the so-called New World, for example. Or the discovery, by three men, of the gene responsible for the dilation of a woman's cervix in labor, a gene to which they now owned the patent. What is the nature of such a patent? O wondered. He had an image of a paper gate around a woman's waist, a kind of chastity belt made of law. The "discovery" of something that is already actively, widely, and freely in use or commonplace, and its subsequent patenting went hand in hand.

I need tissue samples tested, the doctor said distractedly as she wrote on her clipboard, in order to properly diagnose you. O hesitated. He didn't care for the word *diagnosis*; he preferred, simply, *gnosis*. He did not want his life to be called by the name of an illness. And I'll need a complete work-up and a full family history, the doctor was saying, as this could be heritable. History itself is like an inherited illness, O thought. History was like being born telling a lie: you were trapped in a lie that you had not told. Fear was one legacy; grief was another; longing, too. Intertwined crimes seeped in and out of the pores like the radiating wake of a distant explosion, saturating by degrees, mutagenic, stupefying. Depression was a catchall. Sonia had been diagnosed clinically depressed after the dog Violet Ray's demise. She couldn't bear to clean her apartment of the traces of her closest companion. Two days after Violet Ray died, Sonia was startled awake one night by three thumps on her bed, the source of which she could not detect. The experience made her incredibly nervous. She went on medication and only then felt able to vacuum up the hair and the oily residues. As a result of her medication, however, Sonia began to have vivid nightmares of death and waking fantasies of suicide. She experienced several convincing versions of the afterworld while walking around her apartment. The afterworld, she told O, is not exactly a planet, but isn't not one either. Sonia encountered her deceased mother Aletria in the afterworld, where she had asked for help with a crossword puzzle.

At that time Sonia couldn't separate being suicidal from being a mother. She moaned on the couch, Just let me die. O tried to cheer her up. He bought her an oversize button that said *Best Mother in the World*. She asked him how much it cost. He begged her, Mom, please don't kill yourself … because you're a wonderful person. She looked at him sadly. When you were a baby, she said suddenly, your shit smelled like walnuts.

Visibly expanding her rib cage, the doctor exhaled loudly, interrupting O's reminiscences. For the first time O noticed that her torso and upper body were massive in proportion to her tiny legs. She looked as though she could float off the ground. The doctor took off her glasses and cleaned the lenses on the hem of her frock, leaning against the door. Well? she asked.

O said that he would call her but that he had another appointment. She warned him not to wait on the tests. O saw himself reflected twice, oblong in the lenses of her green-tinted glasses. He walked home, pausing once to look at a stand of quaking aspen in the parking lot of a bank. A gaunt man in a trench coat and no shoes stood in front with a sign, *You don't have to be a Rockefeller to help out a poor feller.*

— ∞ O ∞ —

When he got home, O decided to take control. Of what? He would clean, get organized. He found himself thinking of his father as he sorted through and rearranged his few possessions. He had unrolled an old map of Augusta, Georgia, circa 1864, which had belonged to his great-great-grandfather who had died during the civil war. *Powder Mill*, the map remarked, mouth of *Savannah River. Water Works* across from *Canal. Factories*, it went on, *Commons* adjacent to train tracks and *Reservoir. Negro Graveyard*, it delineated casually, bordering the racially unmarked *Cemetery*. O thought of his own father's unmarked grave—the lack of a mark for his father neither masked nor inferred presumptive power. He was, simply, obscure. For O's ninth birthday his mother had surprised him by saying, We're going somewhere special. Thinking of amusement parks and playgrounds, O looked eagerly out the window for signs. They rolled through acre after acre of country. Finally they debarked and walked through a meadow by the train tracks. Eventually they came to a crabapple tree under which, Sonia claimed, O's father was buried. The meadow had a soporific effect, or maybe it was the long ride. She spread out her coat and they lay down to nap. In the late afternoon sun O woke up. He wondered how to distinguish this tree from any other and how to feel in the ostensible presence of his father's spirit. He tied a shoelace around one of the branches.

On the one hand, his father had made sovereign albeit somewhat arbitrary wagers in an arbitrary universe. On the other hand, there was a definite, nonarbitrary design: life was a loan you had to pay back in full. Sometimes your body was taken back from you all at once; sometimes slowly, part by part. Cartographers might map your last resting place, all unknowing, as the site of their own unseeing. Or your bones could lie anonymously, perhaps even fictively in a field. Had his father really died or just changed form, changed direction? O touched the protrusion on top of his head, like an arrow pointing.

He began to reorganize his files. Among his unbearable correspondence, he found a few astrology columns he had saved. He reread an old horoscope. He had circled it at the time: *It is a good time to complete a project you've been putting off.* He read another: *Forgive yourself for every mistake except one —you know the one.* Which mistake? He couldn't say. On the one hand, he told himself, he had no faith in astrology, no understanding of its premises. On the other hand, he *was* a sign, somehow. On the one hand, just as he had four fangs, he was also a Capricorn. On the other hand, to describe himself as a four-fanged Capricorn was to lose touch with something ineffable …

his privacy. Or maybe his freedom. His solitude—crawling thoughts in the dark, patterns and portions of light. Suddenly he thought of what the "one mistake" could be: *Bundles on fire … burning pages.* He had burned his first manuscript, the only copy, besieged by doubt. Doubt, his undoing. How had it come to be that there was such a breakdown between the commonplace way in which one acted and spoke, and the insistent doubt one felt? Doubt was like a shark that constantly circled on the surface of his mind, ready to puncture his thoughts as they glided by. In the same way that he spoke with enthusiasm about astrological signs while what he habitually felt was a droning confusion punctuated by political despair, so too did O seek hypoallergenic pillows when he meant to be writing his encyclopedic, world-historical novel. Was he even more foolish, more hopeless than he had ever suspected? Even as a question mark hung constantly over the idea of astrology, or any such system, O found himself resorting aloud to occult typologies as if he were a committed acolyte, all the while doubting in secret and secretly hoping to arrive at something he could not doubt. By this method, he arrived at doubt. He secreted doubt. Doubt was his rudder. With it, he steered in circles, inadvertently menacing himself.

He supposed the sincerity with which contemporary divinations were discussed—compared to more archaic practices, such as reading the irregular, continent-shaped organs of slain animals—allowed him to indulge in their tautologies (because you are a Capricorn, you are like this; you are like this, therefore a Capricorn) with noncommittal credulity, an indulgence that relieved him of the burden and responsibility of outrage (for if one's problems were a matter of vaporous predestination and not, say, miseducation, well, one could not rage at vaporous fate).

But it would have been false to say that he simply didn't believe in astrology, especially when there seemed to be something genuine in it, in the same way there was sometimes something genuine about a poem. Certain poems, certain horoscopes, certain philosophical texts seemed to recognize their readers. Thus one could be read by what one read. He shuddered. Suddenly he began to cry. To undo the doctor's and Crescent's readings he reached for something else to occupy his thoughts. He closed his wet lashes together and chose from his books arbitrarily, soliciting both chance and providence. His unsteady hands landed on a tattered copy of *Black Skin, White Masks*. In it, Frantz Fanon described the oppressiveness of the white gaze. Colonizing eyes projected violently onto those they lit upon. O thought about his mother's descriptions of childhood, of being hated by strangers, beaten and bullied. Since they did not know her they must have seen evil in her. What was she made of? She wasn't sure. But *it* was there, or why would they hate her? Why would they possess everything, and she, nothing? As a child she developed a fear of having her brain sliced out, inspected, maybe even eaten. Where did she get that idea?

O, the fiction of inevitability on the "face" of things. What would people be like, if they had never been imaginary?

— ∞ O ∞ —

O fell asleep. He dreamt he was in a desert. He had a small, plastic child's shovel and a small broom. He swept the sand. He dug. He was looking for something important, though he knew not what. He dug for a while in one spot, and then moved on to another. Then he found something, a small camera. He turned it on. It displayed a picture of him holding it just as he was. It had a movie, too. In the movie he flew through the night with Skye, Crescent's teacher, and they swam down to the bottom of the ocean. He saw an assortment of rusted implements sitting on the floor of the sea.

She picked up a small screwdriver and screwed it into the top of his head. As she screwed him, he fell in love with her. When he woke up, he didn't remember the dream, but he was excited. He searched for the slip of paper with Skye's number on it and called her.

— ∞ O ∞ —

On the day he went to see Skye, O combed his hair and wore his only suit, heavy iridescent blue with a flared collar. It had been left by his father. Your father was a quick study like you, Sonia told O, but in his heart he was arrogant and mean, a drunk and a hypocrite. On the inside where it counts, she would proclaim loudly, placing O's hand on her heart, you take after me. Sonia had been suing him for child support when O's father died.

O did not think that his heart stood for her and his mind for his father. He knew his mother had shaped his mind, while his heart had a father-shaped hole in it. Or maybe his mind was a mother-shaped hole? What kind of hole was O? He couldn't remember his father. As for Sonia, she cultivated amnesia. But what was clear to O was that in her dealings with his father, Sonia had lost certain romantic ideals. She would never drink. Pills were another story; they were *prescribed*. In any case, O's father left Sonia adrift; he left his son a suit.

O got lost on the way to Skye's. Hot in the suit, he became disoriented and walked in the wrong direction for three-quarters of a mile around an empty, filthy pool, before having to retrace his steps. Skye's office was located in the sub-basement of a nearly vacant building. The only extant business was a teahouse. O walked down to the sub-basement—the elevator was broken—and traversed a concrete hallway that stored dusty bags of sugar and tins of tea along metal shelves lining its walls. O stopped to take a sip from a water fountain.

The steel water fountain, metal shelves, and silver tea tins glared, reflecting the overhead lights. Each tin was thinly embossed with fine-lined birds and flowers. O stood close to inspect one. He squinted at the glint. He looked around; the hallway was empty. He took a tin off the shelf and shook it, expecting to hear the heavy shuffle of tea leaves but instead he heard a delicate ringing like a dead lightbulb. He pulled and pulled on the lid and suddenly it opened. It was empty. How had it made a sound? He put down the tin and picked up another. This one also made a slight clang and ringing sound, as if there was a spring or a little bell inside. He opened it. It too was empty. He picked up another tin on the bottom shelf that made no sound at all and opened it. At the bottom of the tin he saw what seemed to be an ocean. A fish arced out. Her body was propelled back into the water on the downward slope of the jumping curve. But at its upward apex, her outline flew out of the tin and floated past O.

The light off the metallic surfaces made O dizzy. He dropped the tin, leaned against the wall, and slid down to the floor. His consciousness eddied. When the spell had passed, he carefully replaced the tin, stood up and continued unsteadily down the long hall through the tacking refractions.

The hall turned left and abruptly eroded. There were three closed doors. Skye's was the last door O tried, and the only one to open. He knocked and heard a quiet voice tell him to come in. Skye sat behind a desk, preternaturally pale, and blind. When she heard O come in she said quietly, You're late, and gestured to a high-backed chair across from her with a slim wooden pocket affixed to it. Grateful to sit and still disoriented, O vaguely wondered what the pocket was for. In answer to his unspoken question Skye said, It's for a prayer book. The red velvet sleeve of her dress fell back as she lifted her alabaster arm to smooth her milky hair, which spread out across her shoulders like a shawl. After feeling for it, she picked up a tape recorder from near her feet and told O that she would tape-record their session. At the end he would receive the tape. This was included in the price of the reading. He should place his payment in the tea tin to his left. O did so, opening the familiar container. She listened for the click of the lid closing and then pressed the record button. The heavy machine whirred. She asked O what had brought him. He told her about his recurring headaches. She asked him if she could touch his head. He bowed. She placed her fingers gently at his temples and moved them upward. As her fingers searched out the protrusion, O felt warm and calm. He began to feel pleasantly light. Wherever she touched she left a trail of froth. She disengaged gently and asked if there was anything else he wanted to mention? No, he whispered. OK, she said, I'm going into a trance now. She rocked softly in her chair, her marbled eyes sliding and flitting in their sockets.

There was a word for Skye but O couldn't think of it. After ten minutes of quiet in which he gazed at her, trying to remember the word while the tape recorder effectively recorded itself, Skye suddenly asked if he was writing a book to which he responded unthinkingly, No.

She asked him again if he had been writing a book. He found himself saying no, he was not writing a book, that he had been, but he was no longer. He hadn't planned on saying it, hadn't even thought it. But as he spoke, he felt the burden of that ambition dissolve as if an entire city had sunk en masse to the deeps. He could give up on the relentless demands of articulation, fantasies of redemption, research aporias, his health and his larder, the apocalypse, the ambivalence, memories and the odd lack of them, blank pages, novel-writing, pillow-hunting.

If you bring forth what is within you, it will save you; if not, it will destroy you, Skye said. Her eyes rolled skyward as she reached for him. He took her hand. Last year one of my clients found pink hairy stripes growing on her back, Skye said. She is a spider now. O thought he knew why Skye was telling him about the spider, but he wasn't sure. He racked his brain. Taking her meaning made him think of his birth; it *had* happened yet, he couldn't remember it. He depended on other people, specifically his mother, to confirm the fact of his origin. Skye asked him what he did. He tried to answer, but the meaning, the exact details of his working life had withdrawn. His brain refused to produce the file. He saw himself swimming, armless, endless, weaving through dying coral. He saw the legs of a fisherman with a trident and a spear, up to his knees in surf. He rippled past the man, dodging his lunging spear, and then glided back to bite his leg. He said helplessly, I don't know. She nodded and patted his hand. I'm sorry, we don't have any more time; my husband is waiting outside. He thanked her and said goodbye. Outside the room a German shepherd in an orange harness waited patiently.

— ∞ O ∞ —

No, I am not working on a book, he repeated to himself on the way home, and again he felt relief sighing through him. He got off the bus and realized after a confused moment that he'd disembarked at the wrong stop. Across the street he saw a crimson sign advertising Psychic Realty. He wondered, Invisible cities? He crossed the stained tarmac. The sign read Psychic *Reality* after all. A smaller sign, handwritten on a square of redwood, swung on a single hinge. It offered *Palm Readings by Eon* in burnt cursive. He wandered through the threshold. A bell chimed loudly but no one appeared. Feeling awkward about waiting, O opened the first book to hand on the high cedar shelves. He read, *Like everything that has fallen into the unconscious, the infantile situation still sends up dim, premonitory feelings, feelings of being secretly guided by otherworldly influences.*

O heard sweeping from behind an ivory and teak scrim. He walked to the back of the store, peered behind the scrim, and saw an old woman having her palms read by a tall man with the shaved head and calm mien of a monastic. Behind them a teenage boy swept the floor of a back room, gliding in and out of view. When O saw the palm reader, he felt a jolt of attraction. He could hear him murmuring in a deep, low voice, could see a little gold stud gleaming on his powdery soft earlobe. The elderly woman sitting across from him was overcome. Both of her wrinkled hands brown and frail were lightly suspended in his. She shuddered. The palm reader embraced her for several minutes before she left. O approached.

O and Eon sat down on low cushions facing one another. Eon pried O's hands open. The green veins in Eon's ropy forearms rose. O felt the palm reader tracing the threads of his palm with a long forefinger. Eon took his time, studying O's hand with great absorption. O looked as well. He had never noticed the tiny rippling horseshoes and rivulets, so geological-looking.

Finally Eon spoke. Have you ever noticed this? He pointed to a short deep V on O's palm. That's the figure for origin reversed, he said; you will be the last of your family's line. He traced a circle on O's palm and said, The circuit is closed, emptied out. To O's amazement, the palm reader lowered his head and gently kissed O's palms, one after the other. O was electrified. You are the alpha and omega, Eon went on, the instinct and the extinct.

O's mouth was dry. He licked his salty lips. Eon looked at O's hands and nodded as if in answer to a question, though O had not spoken.

O was mounting the weary treads of the stairwell to his door when Crescent's door opened. What did you say? Crescent asked. O stood there on the stairwell looking down at her. I didn't say anything, he said blankly. She looked small and flat to him, like a cutout leaning against the wall, her flowery dress contiguous with the leafy wallpaper behind her. O had the impression of staring at a painted set. He thought about the reading with Skye, which seemed so long ago. There was the reading with Eon, which had left him turned on and sad. Near the bus stop, a few blocks from home, he had seen someone beaten and kicked into the ground by several men. What could he do? He walked past slowly, fearfully, wondering how to intervene. One man turned and said, Can we help you, bitch? O rushed away, trying not to run.

Do you want to have a cup of coffee with me? Crescent asked impulsively. I don't drink coffee, he said. How about tea? He looked up at his door. Or, she said, maybe another time. Yes, another time, he said, thank you. He climbed the rest of the stairs and stepped gratefully into his apartment. He collapsed onto his narrow cot, his grandmother Aletria's old daybed, without taking off his clothes or his shoes. He put his hand on top of his head, which flared intermittently when it wasn't throbbing dully. He rested for a few minutes and then called his mother, who didn't pick up. He thought to leave a message that he was thinking of another visit but hung up. He found himself drifting, thinking about his past, which seemed increasingly fragmented. He tried to think about historical-geographic materialism, a concept he had fastened onto as one he could think with, one he did not doubt at every turn. But just as he had finally begun to feel an allegiance to a way of seeing the world, the idea would waver in and out of focus. He tried to reteach himself what he thought. He felt he was constantly working to retrieve ideas that he had perhaps never fully mastered in the first place; his eyes veered sideways. He looked through his marked-up books, written all over and highlighted with blue ink in a messy scrawl. He read and reread blankly the same sentences; his own annotations were incomprehensible.

Yet segments of history remained vivid in their general outlines, even as concepts blurred. He could picture history: monsters, witch burnings, the Gutenberg Bible. A heliocentric mobile, pumps, telescopes. Encyclopedias, the Haitian revolution, the Declaration of Independence, voting booths, robots. But what was the Kantian sublime again? Was it the knife in his head? Was it Sonia, a professional patient, on line all day at the General Assistance office? The rain? No. Perhaps his fin. For the very reason that it overwhelmed him? But wasn't the sublime supposed to be beautiful? No, the beautiful and the sublime were different categories ... right? In any case, there was no beauty in illness. Was there? But then he thought of his mother's terrible beauty ...

He wanted to see her. He had called her repeatedly. She had not returned his calls. He decided to surprise her with a visit, telling himself she would be happy. He put out of his mind the way she had hated to be surprised when her own mother, his grandmother Aletria, would suddenly appear brandishing crumb cake, the day's crossword puzzle folded under her arm, announcing herself with a startling YOO-HOO that made a person jump out of their skin.

He decided to book a red-eye for the weekend.

He would tell Sonia everything, finally. He would explain. He tried to think of what he would explain, but suddenly he had difficulty comprehending his situation; it slid into fog. He felt out of his depths. Was he already seeing the world differently? He thought he experienced it more elliptically: it didn't add up so much as spread out. It didn't accrue so much as sink. Old hierarchies and chronologies faded and instead there were gaps, undercurrents. In an instant he could know something, but it never coalesced or accreted. Rather his memory was tidal; it snapped into clarity and then smeared into obscurity, retreating like a turtle into itself. Why should it be so hard to think? What schedule was thought on?

He thought of The Thinker, turned to stone, as if to say it isn't thinkers that think, but figures. He sat still, like a statue. He could feel himself becoming a portrait, a caption, a cipher: of patience? Fear? He realized that thought was change; motion. What animal is it that never stops moving? The shark, he recalled, it must always be thinking, agitating the water, seeking.

He had an image of his grandmother, how she walked side-to-side like a penguin, heavy of foot and eye, thick glasses and greasy coat, smoking and cackling, repetitive, content with herself. He thought of Crescent's grandmother, also earthly, a flightless bird. He felt strange as it occurred to him that maybe "grandmother" was a persona.

At that moment he was startled by two knocks on the door.

He was afraid. He remembered the beating he had witnessed. Perhaps they had somehow found him, had followed him. He didn't move. The knock came again, followed by a high, questioning, *O?*

He exhaled and lowered his head with relief. He stood nervously and opened the door to find Crescent, barefoot in a long, peach dressing gown.

— ∞ O ∞ —

Shall I come in? she asked.

Yes, said O.

— ∞ O ∞ —

Lightning struck from an anvil-shaped cloud and clapped them together—a bolt from the blue.

The moon dropped down and rolled around catapulting ribbons of light.

The moon turned into the ocean, the ocean turned into a mouth, and they were swallowed.

— ∞ O ∞ —

The next morning he found a note on his kitchen table.

> *O,*
> *A farewell presence …*
>   *C.*

— ∞ O ∞ —

On the flight to Sonia's O had a window seat.

Surveyor's grids partitioned the surface of the earth into quilt-like panels, the enclosures of agribusiness—square and rectangular patches—ruptured forests, spreading stains, bleeding cuts, and leaking splits. The variously shaped, rhythmically distributed planes of saturated color were scarred by fissures, munitions tests, and mining operations, cracked by winding rivers black and snake-like. Later, the ocean, a thicker, more emotional sky, countless wavelets horned with light, appeared level with the jagged shorelines.

O scanned for reassurance, wishing to feel calm, or sentimental. But whether because of incomprehension—the ungraspable age of a mountain range, for example—or pain—old growth clear-cut—looking at the earth only increased his foreboding. After the sun went down cities resembled nothing so much as motherboards, the rectilinear, thorny grids sparkling with innumerable human-mechanical complications.

$$-\infty \, O \, \infty -$$

The first morning at Sonia's O woke up tired. The old pullout hurt. His heart, too. Would he have let Crescent in if he had known it was only to say goodbye? They had just met. But where was she going? She never said.

Stagnant heat weighted the air. Distracted by his dreams, whose parts he could not articulate, O went to the living room. There sat Sonia, dispirited. What would you like to do today? she asked O. I'm not sure, he replied hesitantly, do you have something in mind? Not really, she said. They sat in silence, listening to flies. He wanted to talk with her; why couldn't he just do it? It wasn't the right moment, never the right moment. She might withdraw.

Finally Sonia suggested they go for a drive. O closed his eyes and lay his head on the back of the other faded purple foldout, part of a matching set. He feared "going for drives." Even the thought of it depressed him. We could go to the park, he said. We could, she said. Or we could go to a movie. I don't know, he said in despair, what's playing? *I Don't Want to Know*, she said; it's supposed to be good. He frowned. I don't think I want to see that, he mumbled. What about the zoo, then, would you like that? she asked. No, he thought. OK, he agreed out loud. To have a preference, he thought, you must be able to anticipate a pleasure. No matter what he did with his mother, he knew it wasn't going to be easy. So what difference did it make?

His gaze lit upon the antique wedding portrait hanging on the wall in front of them. The portrait was encased in an ivory frame detailed with posies and poised little finches. The handsome, thick-boned bride's heavy satin wedding train lay dense and creamy before the couple like a lapping wave. Despite the promising ornamentation in which she was framed, the bride looked dubiously into the camera.

$$- \infty \; O \; \infty -$$

At the zoo there was an elephant doing what at first O assumed was an instinctual dance, her slate gray, finely wrinkled hide rippling like breathing lineaments of stone. She'd walk five feet forward, lift one great foot, swing her head, curl her trunk to the side, drop her head and trunk back down, place her foot on the ground, walk back five feet, and then repeat the pattern. He assumed she was performing an elephant ritual. He had heard of the intelligence of elephants, that they held funerals, that they mourned, and that they listened with their feet. But Sonia disabused him of his fancies, explaining that the elephant suffered from a form of post-traumatic stress syndrome, stereotypy, a compulsion to repeat certain movements ad nauseam. In this case, movements the elephant had been trained to perform while employed by Ringling Brothers. They stared in disappointment. He sensed his mother counting the elephant's steps. Suddenly O yelped angrily, *Ringling Brothers!* He turned abruptly saying, I'll go on. But next were polar bears. One swam in a small tank. The other polar bear suffered the same repetition compulsion as the elephant. It mechanically rocked, nodded, and put up its paw to shake. Sonia had read that the elephant and the bear were being treated with Prozac and told her son this. The same medication as you, O replied.

— ∞ O ∞ —

Sonia and O passed innumerable shouting, eating, tired human families and the occasional caged animal. The polar bear, the elephant, and Sonia had the same problem, O thought. He mentally reopened his dossier and filed this observation under "unbearable correspondence." He visualized dipping a wide paintbrush into a can of white paint and dragged the thick brush over his mother, the polar bear, and the elephant. It didn't work. They emerged through the paint like ghosts through walls, each enacting their own ritual choreography, the bear rocking and extending his paw, the elephant stepping and curling his trunk, Sonia repetitively second-guessing, confounding, undermining, and eliding, rowing her boat in circles. His heart raced acidly. His throat and heart filled with cold blowing air. The insides of his arms grew very hot. Was it her indecision that engendered in him these extreme fluctuating temperatures, provoking a frightening intimation of his own death?

The last night of his visit O's teeth throbbed and his crown ached. He looked into the mirror. He used his mother's hand mirror and parted his hair on top. He turned the mirror sideways. The small cartilaginous growth protruded. He looked into his mother's medicine cabinet for an aspirin. She had Skatterus, Kapitol, Lithalcap, Addvertizorol, Venomind, Panix, Egotrol, Victimall, and a host of other bottles. He found himself pocketing pills from each bottle, two handfuls. She wore a nicotine patch and smoked cigarettes but had no aspirin. And she had sworn off wine. He'd brought a bottle for her, but she declined. I'd rather drink blood, she said.

Why so many medications, mom? O asked. Sonia wandered around the room touching all the surfaces as she explained. My worry machine is turned on and I can't turn it off. That's why I don't like to answer the phone, you know. Your worries increase mine.

$$— \infty \, O \, \infty —$$

When O left this time, the crucial words had gone unsaid. He blamed Sonia: why did she have to be such a mess? So much more fucked up than he was. She hadn't seemed to notice anything different about him, though by now his fin was rather pronounced.

He wondered suddenly what Sonia would come back as. He longed for her to return happy, free of pills, hospitals, and bills. He remembered the zoo. Not as an animal, he thought, no. Maybe an alpine meadow so remote nobody would bother her except occasional admiring hikers and a few harmless sheep, clanging by. Could a person come back as grass? Or music?

He had a row to himself on the trip home, and was grateful. He had blisters on the tops, sides, and backs of his feet. His mother had bought him shoes at a sale. These were supposed to be ergonomic, orthopedic shoes that helped people with back problems, people like him with everything problems, mostly head problems, in his case literally. He took off the shoes; the fact was they were a little too small. His feet were so red. He thought of his mother's feet. Sonia had different colored nail polish on every fingernail and toenail. The nail polish was probably poisoning her liver, he thought. He had read about the toxicity of nail polish, although he didn't understand how nail polish got from the surface of the nail to the liver. He had an image of the liver as this huge flabby fish swimming in the tank of the torso, dreaming of the ocean. But the liver that he imagined in his mind's eye was so large it could not have fit in any human body.

The nail polish is suffocating her toes, he thought, and that's making her brittle and confusing. The little pale windows of her body are being poisoned. He looked out at the unnamed area of sky, framed by his window. That small space reminded him of the square well between apartments where nothing happens but air circulates, and rain comes down, and if you look at the concrete down below you can't help but think, someone could live there and no one would ever know about it. You couldn't pitch a tent, because of the concrete, but you could hang a tarp and have a lot of privacy, which he valued, he told himself. He thought of Tiara Scuro, the blinding fullness of hope that waned to nothing at all. She had left a shard of herself in him, which cut him, as if it was trying to get back to her. He felt trapped in his seat as he forced himself not to think about her, the pills bunching up in his pocket. What to think about instead? The elbow is a wonderful crook, he ventured; the upper and lower reaches of the arm make a perfect mask. If it wasn't for that joint, if my arm was one long bone, he thought, I would only be able to cover one eye against the sun.

After a while he walked in his socks to the toilet. In the raunchy little stall, with its swilling mouth of a toilet, he tried to get into his position, but there wasn't enough room for him to sway. He flushed the toilet and looked down at the spiraling well of blue water on metal, wanting to vomit for a moment, while the toilet itself seemed like an open mouth reminding him of Tiara Scuro's Munch mug. The light refracted off the metal surfaces. Then it flickered, like a strobe. His hands shook. His body convulsed. What's this? he thought. He tried to remember. Leisure? Azure. Measure? Seashore. Seizure! He found the word just as he blacked out.

— ∞ O ∞ —

O awoke with an unfamiliar taste in his mouth, a combination of chalk and unsweetened chocolate. A tiny, white-haired homunculus was sitting next to him on the sink, with a miniature folded newspaper in one hand and a pencil in the other. She was doing a crossword puzzle. He pulled himself up and pushed open the flimsy door. It slammed shut behind him. He staggered to his seat and looked out the window and saw a dark blue river. The homunculus appeared full-size in the seat next to him. She looked familiar. She asked, Can you think of a three-letter word that begins with an O and describes the sun, the eye, a ball, but not a disc? She wore long, Turkish earrings that his grandmother Aletria used to wear. She also wore a black lace scarf with metal sequins exactly like the one Aletria had brought back from Ankara, after she'd visited her ancient father there. O replied, Orb. The homunculus cried, Ah! You always get the right word; that's because you're a writer. She penciled the word in with a satisfied smile. He looked down at the crossword. Orb, written vertically, began with the second letter of the word across, noyade. He looked at her again: it was his grandmother, though that couldn't be, for she had died. Nonetheless, he was enjoying her company much as he used to. He thought, the nice thing about being with grandma is that it is like being alone, but with a better self. What is noyade? he asked. Execution by drowning, she replied. Can you think of a five-letter word, she asked next, that describes objects moving autonomously and interdependently on a plane and on a circuit? Again? he asked. Or is it begin? She stared at him with her eyebrows raised and said, What?

Can I have a hint? he asked. She slowly revolved her fists around each other. Disco? he asked. Close, she said, but remember: a sun, an eye, a ball, but not a disc. Orbit! he cried. She slapped his knee, which he saw but did not feel.

Where are we going, grandma? he asked. She pointed out the window and cackled, Look at the grackles! He looked and saw a flock of black birds with iridescent blue heads ascending out of a wood of sinuous birches, their bark as white as the bird's feathers were darkly opalescent. The birds looked like cutouts, flapping silhouettes. He had the impression that he was looking at a negative.

That he would cease to exist and that there would be no goodbyes had a particularity that seemed fitting. It was as if a decorous heirloom, say, a gray triangle of silk, a scarf that had been passed on through the generations, had fallen unnoticed into a river one day. Carried downstream it got caught on the sharp corner of a creek stone. There it twisted and rippled in the current for a long time, waving and deteriorating slowly, unseen. Then winter came and the silk froze along with everything else, and when the river thawed, the silk was gone, merged with the stone on which it had caught.

My worries for your worries enclose me like a fence around a fence, Sonia had said. Her guilty feelings made her face twitch. It would be a while before she noticed he had not called. The train stopped and he realized his grandmother Aletria had been speaking. You know I'm not talking about our particular family, she was saying, but *Family* with a capital F. How can a tree grow without roots? Drifting like there's nowhere to go, you don't know who you are, and yet your name is Origin.

What does she mean by family? O wondered. If we can't solve the mystery of our life, we move on, she went on. Time will lengthen and grow around our ignorance, like invisible moss, and make something new out of us despite ourselves.

He was startled. Was she hinting to him to start a family? But weren't they both dead? And what about Eon's pronouncement that O was the end of the line? Did the dead reproduce; have families? He had no desire to produce, let alone reproduce. He laid his head against the window and seemed to sleep and yet to wander.

After an indeterminate time, he found himself alone again, the train motionless. He walked through four sets of heavy doors until he found a conductor eating his lunch in the dining car. Excuse me sir, he inquired, where are we? Nebraska, the conductor said. O looked out of the window. Fields of corn rustled in the breeze, their green feathery leaves nestled around the stalk. It's a scorcher, the conductor commented. O went outside to the platform.

A faded poster for a long gone rodeo was nailed to the post beside him. It was a blindingly light day, breezeless and hot. O thought in the history of the *Homo sapiens* it had never been so hot. He looked out and saw his finned head, a shadowy alpha impressed upon an ocean of corn. He stood for a time on the station platform looking at the crops. But he could gather no understanding. At last he slumped down below the rodeo sign and shucked off his corpus, a specter rippled out, heading west to the sea.

THE COFFEE JOCKEY

Dear incomprehension, it's thanks to you I'll be myself, in the end.

—Samuel Beckett, *The Unnamable*

The coffee jockey bent over to get some lids and her back went out. She couldn't move, nor could she speak. People in line just waited and sighed and looked at their watches. The radio played a song by Van Halen. The coffee jockey was bent in half. She could see the rubber mat on the floor, and the shelf where the packets of sugar and extra lids were kept. She could hear Van Halen and she looked at the rubber mat, which she would put outside when she mopped at the end of the day, and she stared at the big holes in the rubber mat and heard the song say, "My love is rotten to the core," and it was like she was being killed. She couldn't stand, nor could she speak. The phone rang and she couldn't answer it. She just hung there, bent in half, staring at the rubber mat and smoking a cigarette. The woman at the head of the line looked down at the coffee jockey bent in half on the other side of the counter and wondered how long it would take to get her espresso.

The people in line were angry about the line and waited impatiently but with a look of patience because of what others might think. They were angry because the coffee jockey made herself a cup of coffee for every single one she made for everyone else and now, bent in half, she had ceased making espressos altogether. One man in line sighed loudly. He crossed his arms and shook his head because time was taken up standing in line. During these interludes he felt his time being wasted. He did not know what to make of this loss, only to lament it.

While the coffee jockey was bent over the woman at the front of the line mourned the loss of precious time. Everyone in line felt time draining away as if the line were a leak. There was a hole where time leaked out, and it really leaked when in line. One man tried to patch the leak with a bemused smile. But eventually the smile would deflate, and hiss back to earth.

To compound the frustration of everyone in line, it had recently been made clear that even though everyone had to work, most jobs were a waste of time. This was making people feel crazy, almost every moment. While appearing normal, their hearts kicked and kicked, invisibly, like the legs of a duck, underwater. "Creating jobs" was the motto, production regardless of need. No one mentioned the possibility of another kind of relationship with mortality, as yet undreamed of.

A man ran down the street. Someone in line recognized his frightened gallop but not the meaning of it, the way one is a body but is unsure what a body is.

The man ran, appeared afraid, and was bleeding. But then he seemed to be laughing. The blood was the juice of a beet perhaps. But no, the blood was coming from his eye. And now he looked very afraid. He was running the way a scared guy runs. Sometimes shouting, "You are an idiot." He tried to pick up an abandoned bed on the sidewalk and threw out his back. He left the bed lying there and limped home.

A man in swim trunks passed him. It began to sprinkle. The man in swim trunks opened an umbrella. A couch fell from the sky. It grazed him, and hurt a little. He ran. The wind was strong. He let go of his umbrella. The umbrella flew away like a swollen, autistic bird.

The line for coffee spilled out of the door. The people in line had small faces and clothes. You could see patches of hair, squares of eyes, and ears. Legs scissored below trunks and heads rotated on tubular stems. Talking and sitting down happened over and over again in the café, in arrangements. There were ponytails and visors.

A woman came into the café. Her hair was yellow and sleek like corn silk, while her roots were dark as earth, so her head was like a vanilla hot-fudge sundae. She was in doubt and didn't know what to do with herself. There was no rest for her. Even ambivalence is too definite a word to describe her state. Every day she asked the mirror, How do I look? She looked in the window to see herself but all she saw were plastic bags in a leafless tree. Superimposed on those in line, her reflection was a collage of impatient stances and expressions.

The coffee jockey, bent in half, had smoked all her cigarettes. One person on line gave up and walked out. She sat down on the couch that had been pushed out of the window upstairs. There was someone else there. "I'd rather sit here than wait in that goddamn line," he said.

There was only one bathroom being used by everyone waiting for coffee. The bathroom door was ajar and a bad smell wafted out. There were twelve buckets of water, catching leaks, and a man with a small radio dancing in there, in front of the mirror. Outside the bathroom a crowd gathered. They watched the man dancing. His hands were like the oars of a rowboat. His torso was erect, and he teetered. He danced like a wooden eel, about to keel over. Another man read his newspaper.

Things were happening in the news about which one could only shake the head. A police officer was quoted as saying, "I've never seen anything so chilling in my seventeen years on the force." The news compressed time so that there seemed to be traumatic events happening every moment of every day. But they happened only once in a while for every person, not too close together, not too far apart. Ill this year, unemployed the next, someone dies, then the car dies, mice on the face, lose a bet, better luck next time, war forever. The reporters kept track of it all until the world seemed to teem more with events than not, and the times when nothing happened went unaccounted for. The wars moved from place to place, outlasting viewers' lifetimes. The line itself shared this quality, snaking as it did all the way to downtown. Traffic was stopped. The coffee jockey, tired from pain, took a nap while bent in half. Another guy in the line bent over to see what she was doing. He looked and saw she was asleep. He stole the cigarette out of her mouth and smoked it there, bent in half. But when he stood up he was a woman. Just like that, the coffee jockey's Virginia Slims for ladies had changed him. He looked down and instead of a dick he had tits. He went home and put on a pink dress. Then he went to play basketball. No one recognized him. He shot hoops for three hours. He found it very meditative. He was a good outside shooter. He was excellent at three-pointers. He whirled around the court and his pink dress caught the late-afternoon sunlight, which glinted in his heavy sheath of hair, and everyone walking by felt more relaxed. He walked home. He felt he had a groin that extended three feet in front of him. He was soon exhausted by his own desire. People cooked with propane stoves in the line, which now stretched all the way to the border. They ate spaghetti and it smelled like the back of a grandma's knee. A tall army guy wore camouflage shorts and sunglasses on a string. He was tired and had given up on having an image. He'd rather never be loved again, he decided, than try to go to the trouble of tricking someone into loving him. He just wanted to be himself, he said. He cut quite a figure when he was out shooting.

Once, he shot his own sneakers. They were sitting on a mat outside the door and he shot them just like that and now he had no shoes to wear. He was walking barefoot and was really embarrassed, trying not to step on glass. He was going to borrow his mother's flip-flops but then he noticed the line. The line was reaching his mother's yard. Now the coffee jockey herself was in line. She cut a figure too, bent in half. She had lost her job after injuring her back. She thought the line was the unemployment line.

It had been so long since anyone had been able to get coffee that even serial killers and telepaths were listless. The line grew and grew. "How long have you been waiting?" the man who had shot his sneakers asked the coffee jockey. "Not long," she said to the ground. "Oh good," he said, with a polite smile. He got in line behind her, not knowing why. Her ass was right in front of his crotch. The toes of his bare feet were in the coffee jockey's eyeline. A vendor came down the road. He would take a picture of you and sell it to you. He hawked his wares. "Keep a picture of yourself outside your own head," he shouted. The vendor was convincing, a master of correct exposure. He came from a long line of bunko operators. His father pulled scams from state to state. His great-grandfather used to lure villagers into his camera obscura. Just outside the contraption, his wife would promenade dressed as the devil, looking consternated. The villagers were pale with fear, for there was the devil, pacing like a thinker, right in front of their eyes.

The coffee jockey decided to have her picture taken as a souvenir. The vendor took the picture, flapped it around with a grin, and in a few minutes it dried. It was blurry but she could tell it was herself because she was bent in half. The vendor was also selling certificates for coffee and unemployment vouchers, so that when you got to the head of the line you were ready. Everyone was buying coffee certificates. The coffee jockey bought an unemployment voucher. Eventually she got an unemployment check from the vendor. But the unemployment check was made out to Rasputin. She wrote a letter of complaint and she got a new check, but this one was also made out to Rasputin.

A cow screamed, abruptly pasted into a collage a teenager was making in line. The cow couldn't imagine how she had appeared there, next to a floating smile, a map of Venezuela, and a lady in a bikini stretched out on an air mattress. The cow had been shitting in a creek, curiously watching a hiker fill his water bottle downstream when she suddenly became art.

Everyone had a particular set of characteristics, sort of like a body type, or a set of emotional ways, and from reading articles you would be able to tell what reasons you might have for killing yourself. You could be in love or have a disease, or not have any money, or be caught in a dragnet or a lie. It was up to you. You lived somewhere ruled by the dream life of oilmen, shareholders, bankers, and eighteen-year-old soldiers. One guy had taken out a life insurance policy on his wife and then plotted to kill her. These were the types of career options in a place like this. He decided he would kill her on a Tuesday. Intuitively, she left him on Monday, at dawn. She drove for ten hours. She finally stopped. She went to a bar but it had just closed so she sat on the hood of her car in the parking lot in the rain. The bartender came out, locked up, and stepped through the line that now cut its way across the parking lot. A cat ran out startled from an open tent waking some of the people who were sleeping in their places. "No cutting," someone yelled from a bedroll. The woman sitting on her car realized it was getting to be night. It had not been night for her for a long time. Why had she driven away from that constant day? She felt she had to and she was right.

All the color drained out of the sky. Now the woman wondered how she might insinuate herself into the line. Her old friend from the salon had a good spot but she would never have asked her to share it because recently, after she'd confided her life story, this old friend had accused her of being depressing. "So you've had some bad things happen to you," the old friend had said, "that doesn't make you special." I hate that bitch, the woman thought involuntarily, remembering equally involuntarily how there had been so much chemical hostility in the salon, that one girl was too disturbed to stay longer than five minutes. This girl had hair on the legs, in the pits, overflowing from above the lips and eyes but she felt it wasn't worth sex to endure the salon. If she couldn't have sex without being plucked, ripped, dyed, and subjected to chemical hostilities then she would masturbate in public. She otherwise felt too much like the chicken just before the butcher broke its wings. She would have enjoyed being eaten if only her skin had not lost all sensation. She got up on the front desk before she left and gyrated in a sinuous dance, her wine-colored locks swirling around her head. She fingered herself. Weeds protruded out of her, sprigs. There was a strange coat of hair almost like steel wool growing around her back. Outside the salon, she mocked the people waiting on line, lifting up her skirts. "Holy Moses," one lifer said, "how about lying under her frilly dress? There's a beautiful portent between those legs." They all saw it and wanted to see it again. They asked, "Are you in the group that prefers the fantasy of electricity or the fantasy of candles?" "Oh, neither!" she replied. "Can't you see mine, how it caves inward darkly?" Stirred up by her fur and her taunts, one man walked out of the line. He walked and he sat down on a stoop. He stood and screamed. He beat his chest. Like a spider he crawled up the air. He had seen a teenage boy who looked like his ex-wife and he was running from that image. It took no time at all to learn to touch a woman, how to smooth her sleeves, have a child. But how could he then forget her? He could not. And his daughter never called. She was in the neo arts and crafts movement. She fashioned condoms out of abortions. She made diaphragms out of Bible pages. She sold IUD icons. She made a film where all the abortions in hell ate cotton candy like there was no tomorrow. She was constipated but not artistically. The pope's soul was hidden in her intestinal tract, she said, and for everyone's protection she wouldn't shit him out until she could figure out where to put it while it decayed, maybe in a barrel in the Pacific by the Farallones along the fault line with the other radioactive waste.

The man who had been hurt by the falling sofa walked past. His hair was green light. He had crossed on a green light, and the green light had jumped into his hair so that soon his whole head was one cone of green light while his torso was a red light and his legs were two blinking, scissoring yellow lights that could go up and down hills. A siren came close to stopping for him. She was enamored; she screamed with a revolving red tongue. All she did all day was run around the city, screaming and rolling her red tongue around and writhing on cars, and this was how she came on to people. Everyone avoided her. In fact when she went screaming by, everyone froze in order not to be seen by her. It was a trick mastered by forest creatures and everyone had learned that holding still is one good way of not being seen. Some had mastered the art of seeming to wander around and shop while slowly dying.

Millions of people could be seen in line, in the paper under a dark screen. They froze in poses of resistance and resignation.

There was an uproar because the dude in blue shorts who sold ether at the mall had disturbed the order of the line by swinging his long arms in big, lacerating arcs of iridescent light that caused people to move out of his way and lose their places. He sprinkled the sidewalk with fragrance and the dogs could smell it, so they too pushed their way through the line barking.

Something was different about the ether merchant. Not his blue-like-an-old-dictionary-blue shorts, but the way he had come out on the surrealist angle of Yahweh. He had no news, only angles. He lived in a basement and he never read a book or a newspaper and he confined himself to watching the sunset from behind the elementary school. The other ether merchant was wearing a long red gown of satin. He hawked his wares that way. He had bottomed out already as a child. There were multitudes like this, killed by death.

A married couple in line looked at each other as if a numb lake had dressed itself in a bandage and called for a party. This waiting was no different from life at home. Their eyes razed each other. They threw each other's clothing down and told each other to watch it. They said, "Turn the clock back; this is too funny." But no one would stop those two hate birds. They did like to have sex, and all the rest of the time skimmed milk. There was nothing else to do, and no one could convince them otherwise. In other words, why would they do anything else, if they could feel uneasy and have sex? They also made food and went on vacations. Even the dog noticed how uneasy they were, and on vacation they were extremely depressed and angry, often murderous. They looked forward to these vacations and brought extra sleeping pills. "Everyone goes on vacation." The dog was like, I don't see the need for vacation. My life is unity.

People waited patiently in line, hoping to be fucked suddenly, either under a painting or, if possible, inside the painting, where the colors would swathe, coil, and transfigure, such as in the benevolent psychosis of infancy. There was a mundane tradition, and then there were these uncivilized rashes of color, and of course colorphobia and wild beasts.

The line continued, in the mind, until it shrank, much as do rinds. To pass the time some people gossiped in verse. They recited: "What was your first impression of him / I often find first impressions are accurate / was it love at first sight? / my first impression was that he was ugly and desperate / a drug addict / I didn't like him / he seemed lonely and dishonest / but we've been together a few years now / and I appreciate all the beer-opener key chains / and the pot / how's your relationship? / oh / we fight / day and night / she doesn't look at me when we talk / when she's in a good mood / I hate her guts / but / we're good / thanks."

The coffee jockey was looking for a roommate. She put up flyers and a toy roommate came to her house and moved in. This toy had bright eyes. He fixed his own hair and he played the piano. He was fond of reciting the poem "are you open yet / no, not yet, but hey, come on in / would you like a cup of coffee / so, how goes it, my man?" The poem was an expression of the toy's preoccupation with the fake transgression of fake rules. He enjoyed pushing the boundaries of literature. If two people were discussing psychoanalysis, or talking of looking at a waterfall, he would be apt to recite (to everyone's face): "what's wrong with you / can't you do anything right / where the fuck are my keys and glasses?" The whole room would light up with pride; this was their toy roommate prodigy.

A girl in line had lost her place and she wouldn't be able to retrieve it now. She'd never been so filled with despair. Her mind was a smashed barge. But then she walked down the street and there, where a pile of furniture had been left, she found a place to sit and be still.

There was a new show called *I Just Want to Fall Asleep*. All you had to do to win was send in a thousand dollars. You'd win a lover. The lover called you and said, "I'm coming to visit you." That was as good as visiting and made actual visiting unnecessary, for the time you would spend together intending to visit would be more enjoyable and honest than the time together visiting, where the attention of one of you would be divided, if not broken, into many unusable pieces, while the boredom of the other was a little flattened tree.

One man had tried to leave his place in line, to "travel." My true passion is the unknown, he said, but he was nowhere near capable of enduring the real boredom inherent in any adventure. His heart ached as he planned a trip, and the trip itself nearly stalled him into total narcosis. The sleepy bitterness of leisure in a distant country was nothing in the end, compared to sitting in one's own chair, turned to meat by the hearth.

But the doctor and his patient decided to take the risk and travel. They were outfitted for frisson and never left their cabin, where they fucked until their very scalps turned blue. One's dick had turned into an iguana. The other's had fallen overboard and, propelled to shore, it took a place in line.

A man sleeping in line woke to the insistent prodding of the dick that went overboard. It pushed the man from the back and the man was compelled to move forward out of line. It pointed him to the sky. The man stood and his leg lifted, then his other leg. The left lifted and bent at the knee, he proceeded forward, then the other leg lifted. In this manner he walked. He placed one foot on the ground, then lifted his other leg and placed the other foot on the ground. But then the ground disappeared below him. He was lifting one leg and placing one foot after another properly, but the ground was not rising to meet him. He had ascended a few feet up as though he were walking up stairs. He walked up this way until he came to a cloud, which he traversed, curiously. But on the other side he fell a long way until no one could see him anymore. Someone yelled, "Hey, you, watch out! There's an abyss there." But it was too late.

To prevent others from climbing to the sky and falling into the abyss, safety measures were needed. One woman was elected to measure the length of the line. She saw that over years and miles objects were getting passed but in the end there was one object that never moved. It faded gradually. Some argued that its fading was a form of moving, but being untrained in scientific method they couldn't prove it. "You are right," replied the woman who had measured, "when something fades it also moves. Therefore what?" And someone shouted, "Therefore something can move without us being able to see that it is moving!" "Yes, good," she said, and so it seems that things can happen in this universe, which you will not perceive. All clapped and wept. But the saying "Your will is not the measure of all things" was greeted with a stupefied groan.

The sky had taken to throwing down tempting ropes and hooks and other things for people to grab on to should they care to climb out of line and take their chances with the abyss. Various people and people and animals took the option and went to live in the clouds and everyone knows they became the cloud people and the cloud animals. They are recognized by schoolteachers and parents as the "pedagogues of dissolution," and children jump out of airplanes to ride them around.

In this way and for other forgotten reasons, more and more people started leaving, disappearing from the line. One after the other, people remaining behind called these deserters to say, "What's wrong? Where are you?" To which the deserters would answer, "I don't feel like waiting." This response was so sensible the line rapidly dwindled away. A few hardcore people stayed. They would wait forever if they had to, though for what they weren't sure. Meanwhile, a gardener planted asters and daisies and datura. She covered her walls in poppies and vines. Her walls were easy to scale if one knew how to crush flowers without damaging them. Animals died and then she'd make them into something fresh to wear, like they did in the past.

But the past wasn't fresh. It was not quite how anyone had pictured it. It wasn't the same. It was no virgin. The past had become distant and jaded. Its painful claims remained indisputable however, for all evil resided there, even the future. It didn't care to reminisce honestly, only to sit and change colors. The past said, "Leave me alone!" But most didn't know where else to go.

One woman wandered away from the line and into a very gross area. There was nothing but crisscrossing freeways and no place to eat, even if she did have money. There was nothing to do but write in her journal or call a friend but she didn't feel like it. She wanted to go on a journey to another planet. There were certain people she avoided, as though predestined. Others she merged with in a fishbowl of understanding until it randomly cracked.

Each person's place removed the possibility of others in it. While there were more people, there were less spots; what would be the criteria for gaining a place? As always: competition. One at a time, through the line, face-to-face, in the round, more blind revolutions. People who weren't getting the job done were passed by. There was one lady who was used to getting passed by. She sat in plastic chair by the highway, eating ice cream, and just watched as the world passed her over in favor of other destinations. It seemed the world had not decided she was a destination; she was only part of the scenery. She had no address, and she produced nothing, so the world had no use for her. She was of no use to the world but she found the world very useful indeed. Without the world, she thought, what would I have to look at?

TRIPLE FEATURE

The movie theater smelled of cigarettes and rain. The rows of seats creaked. The older sister could see that the tall white man on the movie screen was dangerously crazy. She felt sad for him. His flat, wide-brimmed hat was familiar. Who wore hats like that? Oh yeah, the Quaker oatmeal man. The man in the Quaker hat resided where creepy men are found, in bushes by the sides of highways. He was in a terrible mess. Because of his religion. But what is wise blood? This their mother had not explained to them when she took them to the triple feature, just to get out of the house today; she said, "It's only a dollar at the Strand." But the older sister knew that they weren't there to get out of the house, they were there to get away from her mother's boyfriend.

During the movies, her mother kept getting up and going to the lobby. Usually she was rapt at the movies, shushing her daughters. But this time she was distracted. Every time that her mother came back and sat down next to her the older girl looked at her but she wouldn't look back. "Who were you talking to?" the older girl whispered. "Your uncle," she said. "Why?" Her mother didn't answer. The older girl knew that her uncle had lent her mother money. A few minutes later her mother left again.

When the man in the Quaker oatmeal hat poked his own eyes out, the younger one cried and hid in the older girl's lap. He had realized something about life, the older girl thought, something that she knew as well: you had to pay a price. The older girl understood that. She often negotiated the price in bed late at night: "In exchange for him to disappear, I'll wear the same clothes to school every day," she'd bargain. She wore the same clothes to school for a week but it was no good. So she offered more; her hair, her hands, her parakeet. She had no clear sense of whom she was bargaining with, just that it was someone powerful and willing to barter, someone who would accept her pain in kind, even her body parts in exchange for her mother's safety.

By the time *Cabaret* was over, the younger one had fallen asleep. *Barbarella* played next, the only one of the three movies the older girl liked. Barbarella had cleavage like the women in her mother's adult comics. The older one had often looked at those comics. She didn't like the ones with hippies getting stoned and having sex. Those were too ordinary. Her favorite ones were set in a distant place and time. Longhaired barbarians killed monsters and raped women while gods rode by on clouds. The women wore hardly any clothing, at most chain-metal bras, sandals like vines snaking up their shapely calves, and diaphanous veils. She loved Zenobia, Red Sonja, and Belit, each in a different way. Belit was superior, a warrior in leather. Red Sonja didn't hesitate to take revenge, holding her labrys aloft. Helpless Zenobia, in flimsy skirts, gave the older girl a different feeling. She liked to imagine Zenobia chained to a rock, kidnapped by an enormous lizard. She'd slay the lizard and cut Zenobia's chains with her hatchet but not before they had sex, the older girl in her favorite guise as a muscular, invulnerable, but kind and intelligent barbarian.

Her mother had shaken the younger one awake. Outside it was still light. They blinked and caught the bus. At home her mother put on her satin robe and sang them to sleep, *Go tell Aunt Rhody, the old gray goose is dead.* The older girl woke up when she heard him come in through the back door. Then she heard her mother and the man fight, slamming doors so hard her ears rang. Finally she fell back asleep.

The next morning the older girl went into her mother's bedroom but it was empty. Her mother's bedroom had never been empty in the morning before, except last year on the older girl's birthday when her mother and her little sister were hiding with a surprise birthday cake for breakfast. She walked around the house, looking. The house was quiet. She went back to her mother's room. The bed had not been slept in. She pulled back the covers. On the floor she saw a light blue pump. She sat on the edge of her mother's bed, pink foam on a pine plank, and stared at the shoe trying to solve it. She looked at the closet. The hem of her mother's robe was stuck in the door. She tried to open the door but it wouldn't open. She yanked but the door stayed shut.

The phone rang.

The older girl ran downstairs three at a time, flying in a way, and picked up the phone on the second ring. "Hello?" she said, breathless from running, but it was no one, just her uncle. She sat down hard on the stair, dizzy with disappointment. "No, she isn't. I don't know." He sounded strange, or distracted. "What do you want?" She hung up and didn't write down his message.

In their bedroom the younger one played and talked to her creatures. The older girl sat on her lower bunk on the other side of the room watching without seeing. "Where's mommy?" the younger one asked. They heard rattling from downstairs. The older girl catapulted from the bed, ran down the stairs, and opened the front door. The mailman was turning away. She watched him walk, rooting in his mailbag. She thought of following him.

Instead she went back upstairs. Should she call her uncle back? No. He was never any help. Besides she hated the way he smelled and talked.

She went into the bathroom and stood in the tub. She pulled the shower curtain closed and put her hands around her throat which felt as though she had swallowed a burning letter. She had seen her mother burn letters. The younger one came in and poked her finger into the shower curtain. She pressed her lips against the shower curtain and said, "What are you doing?" "Nothing," the older girl said.

The older girl made a decision. "Get your shoes on. We're going to the movies." The younger one ran into her room. She admonished her doll to *stay put* while she was gone. She put on her sneakers.

They went into their mother's room. The older one tried one more time to open the door to her mother's closet. Though she tugged with all her strength, she could not open it. The younger one tried, too. Then she said, "Let's try at the same time." But it made no difference.

They went through their mother's coat. They found some change in her pockets, on her dresser, and a few coins in a can in the pantry. They had a little more than four dollars. The younger girl brought along a small pink horse the older girl had won playing Skill Crane. They got on the bus just as they had the day before. The older girl willed their mother to be on the bus. She glanced around surreptitiously. The bus was filled with mothers, but not theirs.

A man caught her eye. The older girl quickly looked down at her feet. If she looked up, maybe everyone on the bus would be staring, angry. Why?

She didn't know, but she would avoid their disapproval by not looking up. If she did not see them, they would not see her.

They got off the bus and walked two blocks to the Strand. There was someone ahead of them, talking to the gray, bulbous man in the ticket booth. The sisters waited as they chatted idly.

The ticket seller recognized them. "Back again?" he said. They got their tickets and bought one bar of candy, too. Inside the theater the cast of *Cabaret* was singing, "Tomorrow Belongs to Me." The older girl told the younger one to stay in her seat and not move. She searched the theater and the lobby for her mother but she couldn't find her. Then she returned to sit next to her sister, who was talking to the pink horse, ignoring the movie. When the older girl sat down the younger girl stared at her face. The older girl found that hiding her fear from her sister was hard. Like trying to swim with a big coat on.

They watched. The older girl would have been happy to poke her eyes out like the man in *Wise Blood* if only her mother would appear next to her. She'd even be willing to go deaf, dumb, and blind, to be a saint like Helen Keller, a recurring subject of interest at school. Helen Keller was the example of how good and smart you could be against the odds, how you could go without all of your senses, and yet everything would work out for you, maybe even better. You were helpless; the entire world would help.

The older girl wondered what Helen Keller would do in her situation. She closed her eyes and plugged her ears and tried to imagine it. But it was too unrealistic. The older girl felt in the end that *Wise Blood* was more realistic than Helen Keller. But she knew she didn't have to poke her eyes out, not yet. It was enough to show that she was willing. She wondered what her sister could do without. It had to be something important, like candy, or toys. As for her, when they got home, she'd cut her eye, to demonstrate her sincerity. If that was not enough to bring her mother home, she'd do more. They could make a pile of their favorite things and burn them in the yard. It suddenly occurred to her that the sooner she went home and cut her eye, the sooner she might see her mother. She took her sister by the hand and they headed home.

TRANSFORMER

The object of fear is a future set in the past.

—Adam Phillips, *Terrors and Experts*

In the old world, a woman asked her daughter to set fire to the woods with her mind. The daughter tried, hoping to please, as all young do. She looked at the forest behind their house and told it to burn. But the forest remained as it was. "Try again," her mother commanded. "Send yourself into the wood and rub against it with the flint of your life; use that spark." She snapped her fingers and said, "It should catch, just like that." The daughter, obedient, tried again. She closed her eyes and saw herself floating erratically towards the woods. Coming to a broken branch, she rubbed. Nothing happened. She saw the forest floor spread out below her, an alphabet she had only just begun to learn. Her mother looked intently into the trees, scanning for flames. She knew her authority was not in question. Nor did her daughter lack heart. The girl lit upon a small dry twig in her mind's eye and tried to catch it on fire, though she had no real interest in that action, no desire to perform it, the way a dog has no real interest in trying to eat with a fork, except maybe as a joke. What's more, she could tell, though her mother had yet to realize it, that she was not equipped with *that* sort of flint. But she tried. And again, she failed. The mother turned to see her daughter lost in reverie, eyes closed, hands clasped in front of her, her body rising up on her toes, falling back on her heels, a warm, pleasurable pressure in the center of her feet, between her ribs, in her throat. When the girl opened her eyes, she was alone.

She walked to the forest. She noticed a woman in the brush foraging. She also saw a worm moving through the undergrowth. She watched its antenna-like body seeking, telegraphing, worming on. She explored the soft brush of root filaments tangling and expanding, the slow fall of pollen, the light snap of twigs. She sat on the ground writing in the dirt with stems and twigs, entwining them to make stick people.

She had often failed to do as her mother had asked but her mother had never left her before. When she failed to de-bone fish with one smooth undulation of her arm her mother shook her head. When she failed to set off the triggers of guns in the pockets of passing bankers her mother stomped her feet. She failed to attract pollinators and detect gems, expedite the growing season, ward off snow, disease, loneliness, and age, load the dice, win the lottery, or compel with a spell the birch-white Hare to marry her mother, or merely just requite or even stay the night. The girl believed that she did not succeed in these tasks through some unknown fault of her own. She had the vague sensation that her talents had been stolen but she could not allow herself to resent the thief, whoever it might be. The only thing to do was blame herself and she did. She did not even need to believe herself in the wrong, to take blame. She had learned this by studying the archaic wooden Jesus that writhed in the old village church. He was giant, spanning floor to ceiling. Every face in the church, painted or alive, turned towards his bleeding form. The painted people showed the living where to look. They were the envoys of a bygone order.

She knew the story. The continuous, irregular track of the cross, dragged through the desert, would have been like that of a river. Some person or animal encountering the line in the sand might have thought it the track of a very big snake. He took guilt upon himself. That was a relief. Without becoming Christian — that she could never do — she borrowed this technique of self-blame, following the line of the martyr.

Her mother had told her that there was a god for each day of the week, a letter for every location, and a plant for any form of suffering. Jesus had endured, she said, superseding the pantheon, but he was just one among many. Every such entity, her mother asserted, had a time and place, a medicine and a mark, a letter to send. The letter upon which Jesus hung was sent to the place where opposites meet. His time was in the crux between past and future. He was a god known for momentous decisions that altered time. His death signified time's turn, a pivot humans had not yet learned to control. The plant for his suffering was the ash tree. But this was largely forgotten due to the setting down of new codes. Still we live into the future via the shape of a word or letter, she said, which becomes the geography—imaginary at first—of our destination. The girl didn't see the connection. Think if I called myself by another name, her mother said exasperated, would I become a stranger?

From his questions or her mother's responses, the girl had come to understand that the only thing that had compelled Hare to visit, however infrequently, was her potential. Her mother had hidden the disappointing truth from Hare as long as she could, but it soon became obvious: the girl lacked the talents her mother had had at her age. Her mother finally told him. The girl was surprised by Hare's indifference to the news, his unperturbed smile. She thought it was the opposite of what he wanted to hear. Because weren't her talents what he had been waiting for? He went back to the city and did not return.

Her mother's anguish overwhelmed the girl. She watched her lament at the kitchen table, crumpled around a drink, her face unrecognizable, folding and buckling like something that had rotted, lashed like a swathe of fabric in a torrent. The girl did not know what to say to that unpredictable visage.

Her mother's sorrow would crisscross into her and influence her movements. The girl wanted to be on the same side of her own body and hated to be a continuation of her mother's, and so she tried to get away as often as possible. She liked best to sit by herself in the empty attic. She would burn newspapers, cut her thighs, and fill the wounds with ash. She was cutting out the parts of her mother that continued in her, like aberrant organs.

On the daughter's thirteenth birthday they went to a festival. Her mother drank all day and passed out in the rain. The girl rolled her home soaking wet in a neighbor's wheelbarrow. She dried her off and put her to bed. She contracted pneumonia. Confined to bed and unable to get drunk as per usual she grew weak, reasonable, and quiet, lucid as an empty road at dawn. At first she told her daughter stories. Soon she stopped speaking. The girl sat by her day after day. One day the mother said to the daughter, "You don't love me." Dry as a thistle, she perished.

At the funeral relatives and neighbors talked about her mother's youth, a time of silver cutlery, red velvet, grand parties, and aerial duets. If at first her provenance had seemed suspicious—she had had no job or family but owned a house?—her charms soon overcame the community's doubts. She could walk down stairs on her hands. Remember her little old mutt Gangway? She taught him to pirouette. How about when she caught a finch in her mouth? Remember how she repaired the town scale? With a nickel and a pin. Netted the rare iron chrysalis? In a hair-grass rowboat. They admired her at her peak and elided her recent improprieties with that fancy man from the city and his stick-men flunkies. She lived off fame for some time. Her later womanhood proved less noteworthy. She was not fungal, but photosynthetic, one neighbor observed. Her daughter had inherited that at least; look at that moss-green hair. The daughter had not known her mother at the peak of her powers. A natural-born talent, she heard them say. Oh no, she wasn't afraid to shine. Oh yes, she was special. And so she had been, until she was no longer, and then her fame was an ornamental antique about which she was increasingly nostalgic. She had a child that should have brought back the faded accolades but did not.

Hare attended the funeral but he did not speak to anyone. He left right after the ceremony. On his way out he gave the untalented daughter his card. At first she crumpled up the card and put it in the garbage. But then she took the card out and put it in her pocket.

They left the body out for three days; it fell to the girl to wash her mother's corpse. During that time the daughter dreamed every night that her mother had come back, still dead, yet alive. Life ends, her mother telephoned to say, while death goes on forever.

Everything had to be sold off to pay her mother's debts. The daughter didn't care. She did not want any of the clothes her mother left behind, not the teal silk dress with black velvet collar and cuffs nor the tutus, tap shoes, stilettos, nor the romantic silhouettes, dangling earrings, carnival banners, posters of bands, beaded purses, satin slips, boxed letters, framed facsimiles, embroidered robes, stuffed peacock, reindeer antlers, tiger skin, saddles, garters, brassieres, gaudies, mothballs, dolls, or rococo negligees. She took a few things, a random collection of old books; a tiny portable sewing apparatus; a deep, long-handled yard-bag of silk remnants; one sapphire pendant.

The apartment overflowed with well-used but still fine chattel and nicotine-stained scintilla. It became the property of ardent bargain hunters who couldn't believe their luck. Still there were debts. They took the house and asked the girl, What else is there?

The untalented daughter decided to leave. She packed a bag and hitchhiked to the city, without a clear plan. She did not know her way around. Signs of Hare abounded in the downtown area where she debarked from the last ride—his likeness was everywhere. He looked like anyone and everyone in those precincts where accomplishers shiny of buckle were endowed with metronome-like hearts. The people here were pale and physically weak-looking. Hare too had looked weak, thin, but was surprisingly muscular, the daughter had noticed, with a wringing, strangler's strength. Detached or even amused, he and the stick men slit open the bellies of modest rats, hammered the heads of living, signing monkeys and visionary, telepathic cats. They numbered the vivisected organs and catalogued the spliced genes, reducing, reducing, always reducing.

Although Hare had brought her so much pain, and was the reason for the unwanted stick men's sudden appearances, it seemed her mother had loved him. The untalented daughter was impressed by the contradiction. She attributed it to Hare's ability to confuse a person.

On her own she found ways to live. She discovered that while she could not cure pneumonia or start a fire with a glance she was capable of all manner of other tasks conducive to her survival, like trading sex for cash on occasion: fucking was like dreaming, strange and hard to remember. She traveled onward and the past, like the land behind her, disappeared. Which was how she met Lutz, a sometime sailor from whom she did not accept money, with whom she moved in, and by whom she soon became pregnant. She took out her yard-bag and began to stitch a baby blanket.

But they lived in a van. How could they afford a baby? Lutz interrogated the girl: did she have any family or friends with money? She claimed she didn't. He kept at her: how could she be *that way*, if she didn't come from anything?

What way? And he chinned her books, the pendant, the slippery pile of silks, and the evolving quilt colorful as a summer bird. Finally she told Lutz about Hare. She described him as her mother's ex-boyfriend. Fatigued by his questioning she gave him the business card Hare had given her at her mother's funeral. Lutz inspected it. The following day he went alone to see if he might extract some value from the man.

He came to a vast building, an old box store, in an otherwise empty lot. Behind the building on the far end of the lot was a huge white cross in front of an all-but-vanished Wal-Mart marquee. Lutz knocked on a door with no doorknob, waited and then banged with the side of his fist. Hare himself opened, tall in a bone-white suit, his face a sarcastic mask of inquisitiveness. Lutz stepped back surprised. The man scared him. Hare looked Lutz up and down, then set his eyes on the near distance. Somewhere over beyond Lutz's head he fixed his gaze and asked, "What are you doing here, Lutz?" Lutz balked. He glanced back for the source of a steady pounding noise, the echo of a demolition perhaps. But it was only his heart. He had not recognized the sound. But how did the man know his name? He hesitated, then wagered, "If you know my name, you must know I'm your daughter's fiancé." "How can that be," Hare said, "I don't have a daughter." He smiled unexpectedly. Lutz smiled back, confused. Apropos of nothing, Lutz found himself asking the time. Hare thrust his body forward as if to attack Lutz, who jumped back. Inexplicably Hare raised his arms and eyes to the sky and then lowered them to the ground. He yawned and closed the door in Lutz's face.

— ∞ O ∞ —

Lutz didn't tell the untalented daughter of the fruitless encounter with Hare that had begun to obsess him. He couldn't seem to put it out of his mind, which had come alive in an uncomfortable new way. For the first time in his life he began to dread his own thoughts, for they had a life of their own. Having never quite noticed his mind before, he'd assumed he was in control of it. Now he saw he was not; his thoughts were involuntary. He became afraid of language; he felt invaded by it. He found that if he loudly repeated a word or a phrase over and over, or sang, he could partially drown out his thoughts. The untalented daughter tried not to notice.

They traveled around the city together, sleeping nights in his van with mirrored windows, until it broke down beyond their ability to repair. Then they parked it in an overgrown, hilly field behind an abandoned, unfinished residential development surrounded by fences here and there torn open. They lived there as the mound grew. When the baby moved she felt hope, as if its kick augured the return of her own lost promise. But Lutz grew increasingly morose and remote. He was often gone all day and returned empty-handed, smelling of alcohol, vapidly whistling, throwing up, mumbling inchoate verses, clapping, stomping, and shooting cans. She avoided him. The louder he was, the quieter she became. She knew how to turn inward, to become irrelevant, a nontarget. She spun a dense carapace of nonbeing around herself and stayed small. She foraged in dumpsters and fields, and stole food from stores. The more pregnant she became, the more distant Lutz until, on the cusp of birth, he simply disappeared.

— ∞ O ∞ —

The untalented daughter lay alone in a pale green hospital room with two cots divided by a sage green curtain just now drawn back. Above each cot were identical pictures, a wall of trees flanking a kidney-shaped lake. A hawk perched in a birch bent over the water. The trees and the bird were reflected in the lake. Across from the beds a long mirror reflected the pictures. In the bed beside hers was another pregnant young woman. Silently they granted each other privacy as strangers came and went.

— ∞ O ∞ —

Partitioned off by the curtain, the untalented daughter's neighbor was in labor. Her family stood in a semicircle around her. The girl screamed, "Get it out!" They gave her an injection in her spine to numb the pain and quicken the birth. The placenta was caught in a large stainless steel bowl. When the baby slithered out everyone smiled and sighed with relief remarking on its unusual length and squinting eyes. They ignored the bowl of blood and meat which was set to the side. It was full of kaka, a bloody crumpet-like plakoenta the untalented daughter observed, though no one partook of afterbirth anymore, she knew, resorting instead to symbolic cakes.

— ∞ O ∞ —

The girl across held her newborn baby, uncoiled and quiet as a snake. The family prayed nervously, "For blessing us with this eel of a child, we give thanks." The newborn breathed gravely. The placenta was discarded.

In the other bed, scheduled for an imminent labor appointment, the untalented daughter thought, "I shouldn't let that kaka go to waste." Her nerves began to stand on end with the onset of contractions. She felt the slow whip of it and admonished herself. The bellows took her by grim surprise. "*Prodigious motion felt and rueful throes … all my nether shape thus grew Transformed,*" the masked medic recited, injecting her with precision.

Thereafter she felt nothing from the waist down, though the gap where the agony had just been was alive, its very cessation vibrating with the recollection, the tertiary trace of a sirening fire engine trying to make a U-turn in her one-way street of a cunt.

Her baby was born in the time it took her mother to get drunk on an empty stomach. She named the baby, birth-bruised as blue dusk, Lutz Junior. When she awoke, she was alone. The new mother ignored the forms next to the bed. She retrieved both placentas from the toxic waste receptacle and, triple-bagging them, hid the meat cakes in her complimentary diaper-clutch. Moving carefully so as not to be seen, she ducked past the high desks, the machines, and the uniformed medics. She walked home holding her baby tight.

$$— \infty \, O \, \infty —$$

The new mother cut and dried the placenta cakes. Lutz Junior grew strong over the years, nourished by breast milk and the rusty, sweet, nutrient-dense meat cakes of two births. "A piece of heaven," said the little girl of her daily ration. The blue van with mirrored windows was sufficient shelter. The new mother did not miss Lutz. His presence had been lonelier than his absence. Lutz Junior was companion enough. As her mother had before her (*your father was made of glass; he shattered*), eventually she would contrive a fable to tell Lutz Junior about *her* father.

She relished her daughter's spontaneous dances. Her heart flushed a sweet jet. She brushed her daughter's naturally droopy, slick grass-green hair until it feathered around blousy as a flower. In turn, the little girl combed her mother's thin, moss-green hair. Her mother read to her and told her stories.

Lutz Junior could climb anything and once held a hummingbird lightly in her mouth. She was mesmerized by the nest-building afoot in the trees, the leaves overhead threaded with red, blue, and yellow wings, leafy little branches held fast in small beaks. They picked wild blackberries growing along unminded property lines, careful of thorns and rusted barbwire in fields crowded with dandelions. They found clay on the banks of a red river and brought it home. Lutz Junior fashioned little figurines of birds, her mother, herself, trees, and a clay alphabet.

They spent much of their time outside, foraging, stealing, walking, and playing in the scattered fields, lots, and streets. Collapsed buildings and the fading away of "developments" had enabled edible plants to return to untended lots and abandoned houses, where they grew enthusiastically and were harvested and sometimes cultivated by the canny and displaced. One day Lutz Junior asked her mother why she was named Lutz Junior. Her mother told her the unsimple truth, "You're named after your father, a sailor." She brought out a book of knots that Lutz had left behind. The young mother wrote a dedication on the first page, *For My Daughter To Untangle, From Her Loving Father.* Lutz Junior pored over it and studied the knots with interest. "Knots remind me of letters," she said. "Where is my loving father now?" she asked. "Your father disappeared into the past," her mother replied. This made sense to Lutz Junior. For where was yesterday? The past was like a hiding place almost impossible to find. Therefore she was satisfied with the answer.

She tried to go back there. Though at first she thought she might have located the outer border of the past, she could not pass through it. She had gone intending to walk back to her own beginning, and had come to a high wall. The wall was concave at the bottom and opened out way up at the top, like a wide funnel. Even if you managed to climb to the top you would still have to find a way to get over the cylindrical lip of the uppermost portion of the wall, which, improbably thin, sailed vertiginously outward, an enormous petal. Lutz Junior admired the wall. She climbed the highest tree but still could not see over it. It suddenly occurred to her that perhaps the past *was* beyond that wall; perhaps her father was there. "No, *that* is the future," her mother explained, pointing to the diamond-alloy border wall beyond which lay who knew what forms, what knowledge? "How do you know?" Lutz Junior asked. "Because the past is something you can feel, but not touch." As to whether her father might have meant to hide there or had gotten lost, Lutz Junior's mother was incurious. Lutz Junior made a small clay replica of the wall, duplicating its sweeping concavity, carving with the curved back of a spoon.

— ∞ O ∞ —

The untalented mother got a job at the snack bar at the train station to pay for schoolbooks and clothes—she intended to send Lutz Junior to school. The girl would play in the wide echoing waiting area. She learned the routes and the names of the trains. She saw people stand in pensive postures, check the marquees and their watches.

Existence at the station took the forms of waiting, staring, and then filing, walking, or running down to the tracks when the train came into the station. How distraught they became when trains were delayed, or if they themselves were too late, sometimes crying or yelling. How reassured they were to be met. Her mother called them sir and ma'am. Lutz Junior learned to do the same. She ran up to other children sometimes. Right away they met as comrades, learning each other's names and falling into play. They were absorbed by one another yet sanguine when they parted. Sometimes she made the acquaintance of older people. One elderly woman smiled kindly at Lutz Junior. All of her possessions were bundled into plastic bags. She was not waiting for a train, she said, just taking shelter from the rain. "Do you want to hear a riddle?" she asked Lutz Junior. The little girl nodded. "What passes but never passes; is the traveler and the traveled; abides but doesn't exist; makes everything and destroys everything?" Lutz Junior didn't know. The woman said, "Do you want to take a guess?" But Lutz Junior couldn't guess. The old woman pointed at the giant station clock. Lutz Junior understood; time was shapeable but also beyond shape. Not like clay; more like thought. For while clay could only represent time's passage, time could destroy clay. You were shaped by time, like ideas, but would not find the end of it.

On another occasion Lutz Junior saw a pale man in a white suit outside the station looking at the sky. She went closer to him and asked him what he was looking at. "Hawk," he said, pointing. She saw a big bird with reddish striped wings swooping over the station. "I've seen that bird before," she said, "I didn't know it was called a hawk." "What did you think it was?" the man asked, smiling. "I didn't know." "Did you have a guess?" he asked. "No," she said. He laughed. "Good for you, you don't make things up, do you? Who cares *what* they're called, right?" He glanced sideways at her and resumed his bird-watching. After a moment he said, "I'm called Hare, what about you?" But Lutz Junior was still thinking about what he had said earlier. "Your name's not Hare," she said. "OK," the man said slowly, "then tell me, if you think you know, what's my name?" The hawk flew a little closer and circled before landing gracefully on a street lamp. Lutz Junior looked at the hawk and heard her mother calling her name. She looked back at the man but he had gone.

— ∞ O ∞ —

The untalented mother was determined to improve their situation. She taught Lutz Junior to spell; with diligence and quickness of mind she was soon writing. The mother tried to white the green out of her own hair, but the speed bleach just made her hair fall out and it grew back algae green. "Why is your hair like that? What are you, a punk rocker?" her manager asked. "No," the mother said, "it's not deciduous." "OK," he said, "but you're *American*, right?" She wasn't sure what to say, but luckily he didn't wait for her answer. "Just try to fit in," he said.

The mother wanted to fit in. She wore a white beret left unclaimed on a bench in the station, to cover her recalcitrant hair completely. From her time in the sex industry she knew how to put on makeup. She began to wear it to work. Watching her mother do her face, Lutz Junior held a jar of cover-up and asked her, "What's this for?" "It's cover-up, to make up my face," the young mother answered. "Like make believe?" Lutz Junior asked. "No, it's not pretend; it's makeup—that's different," her mother explained. "When you make up your face, it's to show you're a real lady." Lutz Junior considered this and asked, "Will I be a real lady?" Her mother smiled. "I don't know," she said. "Do you want to be?" Lutz Junior said, "No." "That's OK," her mother said. After a few moments of watching her apply mascara and eyeliner, smudging it, cleaning it off, and then reapplying it, Lutz Junior decided that it was a boring game. She didn't want her mother to play. She asked, "Are you sure you're a real lady?" "Of course," her mother answered. Lutz Junior watched her mother's face in the reflection. "No, you're not," she said. The young mother frowned. Anxiety undulated through her suddenly clouded mind. Lutz Junior saw it. Her mother had shown her yet another face, as if the one she knew had momentarily faded away. "Can we play five-card draw before work?"

Lutz Junior asked, wanting to change the subject. She crawled under their bed to fetch cards out of a shoebox where she kept her toys and three partial decks, which combined to make one full deck of playing cards. The untalented mother lit a cigarette. They played. Sensing her unease, the child let her mother win.

— ∞ O ∞ —

One day Lutz Junior saw a moth in the station. It floated above her making its way seemingly at random. She followed it with her eyes until it landed on the marquee where the train lines and arrival times were announced in movable metal type. The moth walked across the letters. Lutz Junior heard the soft clicking of its feet as she watched the moth. It felt as if the little moth was striking matches in her heart. It made her want to laugh. The moth landed on the letter O. Lutz Junior smiled. O was her favorite shape. It was a letter, a number, and a picture all at once. Sending up her mental hands, she disarticulated the letter from its setting and floated the O, big and soft as a peony in bloom, so that it was all by itself, a lonely halo hovering over all the other letters on the top line. She slid the letters in and out of their old slots and into new ones where they snapped satisfyingly into place. She visualized her mother's name, hard, translucent resin and a livid red compass. In her mind's eye this was her mother: ancient resin and pink fire. Her own name was a little lantern. Soon she had spelled out her mother's on the small station's single marquee.

She petted a feral station cat while a small chaos built up below the marquee. People looked at their tickets to assure themselves, though they already knew, that though the scheduled departure time was the same, theirs was not the Amber Rose line.

Lutz Junior was surprised by her mother's panicked response at seeing her name on the marquee. The prank, as he called it, tried her boss's comprehension. "We're going to have to let you go." Amber Rose did not hold Lutz Junior's hand as they made their way home. She did not speak to her as the child cried, confused. Amber Rose did not bother to ask Lutz Junior how she'd done it; she knew and it filled her with dread.

— ∞ O ∞ —

The reverberating, muted voices, simple, detached transactions, and anonymous cries of the train station had been soothing to the untalented young mother. She grieved the loss of her job in the church-like, echoing room with its sloping walls, worn wooden floors, and domed ceiling. The old sensation of her mother's parts and sorrows crisscrossed in her, continuing themselves like unwanted organs. For Lutz Junior clearly had the talent *her* mother had expected and wanted from her, and though she herself had created Lutz Junior, had nourished the infant exceedingly well, her child's sudden, unbidden demonstration of talent evoked in her a rage that she had not known she was capable of. She saw now what a disappointment she must have been.

One day Lutz Junior spelled out her mother's name by hand on the ground outside of the van with stems, leaves, and flowers, just to see what would happen. She formed a small stick mother and a stick child holding hands beside the name. Clouds bundled together overhead as if to watch. When she saw her name spelled out like that and the stick people, Amber Rose slapped the child, after which Lutz Junior set her own small spiral of hair afire and the clouds drifted helplessly apart.

At first, in the weeks that followed, the girl would turn it in on herself that way, but soon, without having intended it, on both of them: small burns on the feet and hands, involuntary kicks and throws. The mother despaired. Just as Lutz Junior could not control her burgeoning power, Amber Rose could not control her rage. Her own mother had stranded her, but eventually, through Lutz Junior, Amber Rose thought she had recovered her ground. But now she saw that the road that she thought had moved forward was going back. It would not be possible to go on after all. The pattern of succession would elude her. Lutz Junior could see that, in some way, she had gone beyond her mother. She was no longer trusted. Sometimes her mother looked out the window and spoke to it as if it was a person. To whom was she speaking? Was she looking at someone that Lutz Junior could not see on the other side of the glass?

— ∞ O ∞ —

Lutz Junior took to sitting outside high in a tree she had climbed before she could write. She watched the van from there, observed her mother coming and going. She no longer returned from her outings with bread, milk, eggs, potatoes, cornmeal, apples, and candy, but always with a jug of pale wine.

Amber Rose's face grew gaunt and structurally distorted, her jaw listing to the left from a kick in the face that knocked her down and flung her front teeth to the ground. The internist at the free county hospital felt a vague dismay—who had done this?—but she did not ask, trained against entailments. She simply put the teeth back in, where they did not reroot, so the mother's two front teeth became a smoky little set, two static screens.

One idea took hold of Amber Rose's mind and traveled its track repeatedly: perhaps Hare would give them money. He'd want to know about Lutz Junior. Her own mother had greatly interested Hare at first. Her mother had been in love with him. Then Amber Rose herself had interested Hare, until he found out that she had no talent. Lutz Junior *did* have talent, though, and Amber Rose assumed Hare would want to know. Recoiling inwardly at first, she convinced herself that he would care, that he would help them. She forced herself to think the thought until it ceased to sting. The idea became a plan. She began to think of it as predestined, a task assigned to her no different from restocking the sugar, salt, tea, and coffee at the station kiosk, no different from any other burden she had to carry. She did not let herself remember that it was her idea, for if she had she might have doubted herself. She acted as if it was an instruction given her from outside. For if it was someone else's decision (whose?), it was only for her to carry it out. After all, she herself had only ever had one special capacity and that was to worm away, to worm out, and that one talent remained. For the rest, she was only another survivor with a mind like a midair explosion. She cut herself and picked the scabs. At night when she slept, Lutz Junior crept close.

The child berated herself. She did not have the power to undo what she'd done, or what she had become. She had ruined everything. She had not known the rules. But now she would be vigilant. She must not make any more mistakes. She would not spell names; she would not play games. At night Amber Rose felt the child sidling up next to her, a small warm animal, and she turned her back.

— ∞ O ∞ —

Lutz Junior and her mother, skinny and bony, mast poles tilting right and left in snapping gusts, set out one afternoon. She held her mother's hand tightly as they whaled along, rounding the corner of present time. Until that day Lutz Junior had always experienced life as forward motion. Her mother's silence, though nothing new, was unusually heavy. Lutz Junior asked where they were going. Her mother said, "We're going to visit someone who can help." Help what? Lutz Junior wondered. She kept stopping to pick a thing up, trying to delay their momentum. From her mother Lutz Junior had learned that the street provides: nails, plastic cutlery, and umbrella bones, rubber bands and stale bread, caps, bottles, and butts, rotten fruit and bruised shoes.

They stopped at a corner store for cigarettes. The man at the corner store was friendly. "Sisters?" he asked. Amber Rose said, "She's my daughter." He shook his head with amazement. Lutz Junior felt proud. She liked the man. Her mother distracted him. Stealing was easy if you had good will. In any case one must find a way, a method, and Lutz Junior was a good improviser. While they were in the store, Lutz Junior's nervousness subsided. She wished they could stay in the store talking and stealing forever. She fantasized about moving in with the storekeeper. They would watch his little television and eat his candy. Amber Rose put down two dimes for a pair of cigarettes sold loose from a can. She showed the clerk an old dilapidated business card and, after cautioning her that it was far, too far to go on foot, he gave her directions, drawing a little map on a scrap of paper.

Lutz Junior had a couple of candy bars and a pack of gum in her pocket by the time they left, which she handed to her mother once they were out of sight. A black-and-white spotted dog joined them for a while, rushing along beside them earnestly as they walked through shortcuts behind abandoned buildings, across polluted intersections, below ramps snaking like tails and glistening like scales with cars stuck in traffic, across railroad tracks, through the parking lot of a great, closed school of pale orange bricks. They came to a hilltop view of the sea and they paused. "What is it?" Lutz Junior asked. "The ocean," her mother replied. "Humans come from there," she added. Lutz Junior pointed again, asking, "We come from there?" Her mother said, "No, not *us*." "Why not us?" Lutz Junior asked. Her mother said nothing. "Can we go down there?" Lutz Junior asked. Amber Rose's heart suddenly sagged with fear and doubt. What was she doing? Hare had always mattered more to her mother than Amber Rose herself had. But why had *she*, Amber Rose, mattered so much to Hare? Who was Hare?

Amber Rose remembered that when her mother had finally admitted to Hare that her daughter had no talent, Hare had not looked disappointed: he had looked glad. It made no sense. For a moment, Amber Rose hesitated. She thought of taking Lutz Junior to the sea as if it was their destination all along, then taking her home. Just then Lutz Junior asked again, "Why not us?" Amber Rose said, "It's too much." "What is?" Lutz Junior asked casually. But she could not keep the worry from her voice. She could avert her eyes, even her thoughts, but her voice was naked. Abruptly Amber Rose resumed walking. Lutz Junior waited. Would her mother turn around? No. She didn't look back. Lutz Junior ran to catch up.

They continued onward. Lutz Junior noticed a line of ants crossing their path and jumped over it. She saw a clothesline with old stuffed animals dangling by their legs and arms: a faded blue bear, a smudged pink pony, a flattened frog with no eyes. These sights distracted her. The question of her origin and the sea hovered in the background, to be pursued later when her mother might be more receptive. They passed a flock of pigeons that wheeled out from a rooftop. Lutz Junior turned and saw them return in a cascade settling back in errant, distracted patches like people at an open-air market. She saw facsimiles of predator birds and wondered what they meant.

— ∞ O ∞ —

Amber Rose and Lutz Junior came to a large building all by itself in a vast lot. Behind the building on the far end of the lot Amber Rose noticed an enormous cross. She remembered a fragment of her mother's story about the crux, her own childhood adherence to the path of the martyr. She recalled grinding her mother's coffee, blending her drinks, purposely going outside in the cold with no coat on to see how long she could stand it. Her face was wet. She didn't notice but Lutz Junior did; she drew closer and put her arm around her mother's waist. Amber Rose pointed to the cross and told Lutz Junior, "That's the letter that stands for tree." Lutz Junior looked at the converging lines, sounding out the four corners described there and read the sign mounted above: *Global Corps./Timeline*. "We're here," Amber Rose said helplessly. Lutz Junior looked at Amber Rose. She could tell her mother was upset. But was she afraid or angry? She watched her mother spastically lift one foot, wrap it around her other ankle, and chew her lip. She took out the crumpled-up business card Hare had given her so long ago and held it out like a ticket. She smoothed her hair with her thin, flat palm. They ascended a few stairs to a door with no doorknob. The untalented young mother turned to Lutz Junior, who composed an expression of careful attention, a mask that pacified her mother who knelt down and pleaded with Lutz Junior to be good. "Promise?" she begged. With shame and sorrow, Lutz Junior realized her mother was afraid of her. "I promise," she vowed. Her mother stood. She rested her forehead on the thick door for a moment before she knocked.

Lutz Junior recognized the man in the white suit who opened the door. He greeted them with a noise of general surprise. He patted Lutz Junior on the top of her head and said, "Hello again!" Lutz Junior quickly put her hand on her head where he had touched it. It felt as if he had left something lying there. Amber Rose looked at her daughter and back at Hare anxiously. "We met once outside the train station," Hare explained. He smiled at Lutz Junior, showing his teeth.

Hare escorted them into a large room filled with stick men working. Some performed repetitive movements in torpor. Some sat at desks, some consulted charts, others stood in clumps talking restrainedly, others walked in and out glass-eyed. A few sat on a long bench bisecting the overly lit room, watching monitors and clicking. The pervasive drone of machinery made voices hard to hear. The stick men appeared uniformly worn out. They soldiered on. The air was stagnant, no windows. The floors glared with dull gloss. They struggled a little for breath, as if there were diminished levels of oxygen in the room. The very air had withdrawn.

Amber Rose seemed tired, discomposed like everyone else except Lutz Junior and Hare. "Would you like something to drink?" Hare asked, his eyes bright as he glanced back and forth. Amber Rose declined. "Is there somewhere we can talk?" she asked. "Of course," he said. "Why not have your daughter wait in here. She can help the monitors if she likes." He smiled and pointed to the long bench in front of a grid of small screens. Amber Rose looked around at the stick men with atavistic revulsion. The one nearest to them had a leaf-shaped birthmark under his left eye, like a coffee stain, all the way to his jaw, and his forehead was covered in thick wrinkles. He raised his bristling eyebrows in friendly greeting to the child, and with the air of a simple invitation, he patted the area next to him, inviting her to sit. Amber Rose pointed Lutz Junior towards the bench. Lutz Junior said, "But I want to go with you." "I'll be right back," Amber Rose said, loosening her grip. But the little girl wouldn't let go. "Remember what we talked about," Amber Rose said grimly. Lutz Junior dropped her mother's hand instantly and mentally renewed her promise. Amber Rose turned to leave the room with Hare. "Tell me about her," Hare said as they walked. "What is she like?" Lutz Junior sat down on the far end of the bench. She turned her head to see the door close behind Amber Rose and Hare. She could hear their voices at first, then nothing. She sat on the edge of the bench and her eyes wandered from one lively flat surface to another.

On one screen she saw scratched footage of a village procession of people and animals winding down a narrow, spiraling mountain path carrying the Virgin Mary in a covered box garlanded with flowers. Men playing trumpets and drums and a little girl in long gown and tiara carrying a heart-shaped red pillow were followed by a lamb with a small bell around his neck. When the pilgrimage reached the bottom of the mountain they began to ascend, in this way continuously looping around the mountain. The chaotic line of journeying people, scattered talking, and dissonant singing reminded Lutz Junior of the train station. On another monitor a man in a nightgown with a thick mustache and black glasses tried to figure out if the likeness he saw in a giant mirror was his reflection or an impersonator. He tried to outwit his reflection. Unknowingly, however, he crossed to the other side of the mirror and became his own double.

On another screen a commercial showed a well-dressed couple in a new car listening to a song. Everything on the other side of the windshield of their new car occurred in perfect rhythmic accord with the song. The gestures of shop clerks, the sweeping movements of garbage men tossing bags of trash, a few oranges spilling from a produce stand into the street where street cleaners swept and a boy skated by—all was in synch with the song. The couple watched the animated bas-relief around them with cool pleasure and approval from behind the windshield.

Lutz Junior glanced at the monitor above and was surprised to see a familiar woman and an even more familiar-looking child, standing together behind a house. She immediately knew that the little girl was Amber Rose. The pair faced a forest. The child bounced ever so slightly up and down, like a bird on a branch, as if the ground beneath her feet was bending and rising. They looked at the trees in silence. The woman glanced back at the girl once, and then resumed scanning the forest. Suddenly the woman turned and slapped the child. The girl's face turned for a moment towards the camera lens, so that it became visible. The woman hit the child again on the head. The child raised her arms self-protectively. Then the image cut to the child petting a small black cat. A stick man in the scene pointed at the cat and said something. Suddenly the cat's face distorted. The girl was crying and strangling the cat. The cat snarled, scratched, and ran away.

Anxiously Lutz Junior stood. A couple of stick men glanced at her and then looked back at their monitors. She asked the nearest ones if she could go to the bathroom. She didn't really have to go but she desperately wanted to leave the room and she needed an excuse. One pointed towards the hallway she and her mother had come through. The second door to the right was the bathroom. She headed that way. She had not noticed before when they had come in that there were so many doors in the long hall. There was even another, smaller door right beside the front entrance.

Lutz Junior went into the bathroom. She wanted to wait there until her mother came and they could leave. She sat on the toilet but nothing happened. The image of the woman and the child played before her eyes repeatedly as if her mind had become a television she couldn't turn off. She saw the woman's face and the child's face over and over. She climbed up onto the sink and looked in the mirror inset into the medicine cabinet door, to see if she looked like the woman and the girl. It wasn't her first time looking in a mirror. But something was wrong with this one. There was nothing there. Her face had gone. She had seen its semblance inside the woman and the child on the television. Everything that was secret in her could be seen in the faces of those others, but was not to be found in this mirror, which did not reflect her.

In stories some mirrors had an autonomous existence, wills of their own. Perhaps this was one of those? Without her face to look at, her surroundings became more important. She looked down at her legs and feet. She looked around the bathroom. The room seemed unusually vivid. Her surroundings were what were left to remind her that she existed. They existed because she perceived them. She existed because she perceived them. She existed because she was perceived: but how was she perceived here? She could see there were different rules in this place. She didn't know what the taboos, tests, roles, and requirements were and she didn't want to. She only had to abide by her promise to her mother.

She looked again in the mirror. Her own face could not remind her that she existed, because she could not see it, but she could see everything else in the room and in this place, and she wanted all of it to be erased. She looked down. Her feet looked strange to her. She remembered her mother leaning down to tie her shoe and then seeing her own foot involuntarily kicking out and her mother falling back and then two teeth were on the floor. Lutz Junior picked up a tooth with her small fingers. It was bigger than her fingernail. She staunched and iced her mother's bloody mouth. Her mother had cried. Lutz Junior did not understand why her own foot had kicked out so strongly at her mother's mouth. It seemed like her mother had kicked herself by means of Lutz Junior's foot. Lutz Junior had felt that way before. She sensed that her mother used Lutz Junior's body against her own. And yet she also understood that Amber Rose did not know that. She blamed Lutz Junior, and so Lutz Junior followed suit. Everything was easier if she took the blame, the details didn't matter. She came to understand that love was not the same as justice. She would live as an infinite apology, and perhaps someday she would be forgiven.

She walked around the edges of the small room. She turned the faucet on and off. She counted the tiles on the floor. She saw a moth which reminded her of the moth that had landed on the marquee at the train station and caused so much trouble. She knelt down. She picked it up with a finger and the moth turned to look at her. She touched it lightly to her lips. The moth flew up to the window.

She heard her mother's voice; she and the pale man were arguing loudly. Lutz Junior cracked open the door to see with one eye that, incredibly, her mother was being shoved through the door *without her*. She saw Hare turn the lock.

While his back was still turned, Lutz Junior stealthily closed the bathroom door. Was he trying to lock her in? Her heart pounded; her innards went slick and hot while her skin felt icy. She stared around the bathroom not knowing what she was searching for until she saw the window above the medicine cabinet, cracked one-third of the way open. Quickly she climbed onto the basin of the sink and, carefully balancing on its edges, pulled her weight up from the ledge and shimmied on her belly out the window until she was on the external sill. There was a drainpipe. She slid down it scraping her knees and hands bloody and in moments found herself panting by the side of the building.

It was dull-skied and quiet, the air thick and still. A statuesque, clean-winged pigeon stood next to her. Lutz Junior ran around the front to look for her mother but no one was there. At once she realized that perhaps the small door next to the entrance that her mother had been pushed through had not led to the outside, but to somewhere else in the building. She heard a noise like a thousand locks clicking. She ran towards the door, startling the pigeon into flight. But the door had melded into the walls. She couldn't see it, let alone open it; she couldn't even find its seam. Suddenly a deafening siren sounded; mindlessly she ran away.

— ∞ O ∞ —

She ran blindly from the alarm, until she couldn't anymore. She thought to retrace the path back. But though the way was familiar, she didn't recognize it exactly. She remembered jumping over a line of ants that had been crossing a square of the sidewalk in front of her; a clothesline with stuffed animals hanging from it; the glittering ocean. She did not know how many times they had turned, whether they had turned right or left, how many hills they had walked up or down, or the names of any of the streets they had taken. She never mapped the routes they took, but left such things to her mother.

Just then she saw a flock of pigeons wheeling ahead. She stopped, arrested. This was familiar. But it was not the same flock, not the same building she had seen before. The pigeons landed, then rose from a rooftop, swooping over her head as if thrown by a single hand. They circled back to their roof, ignoring two kites that flapped there in the shapes of an owl and an eagle. They were becoming hard to see. The light was draining out of the sky.

She wandered, viscerally apprehending the reality of her abandonment, a widening fissure that was not there before. She glided in a fume of fear feeling something irreversible forming she knew not where.

— ∞ O ∞ —

Lutz Junior came upon a bench hidden behind a tree, on the incline of a weedy hillside. Fatigued, she sat down and closed her eyes. She saw her mother's face, then Hare's, the O on the marquee at the train station, the sea she'd glimpsed and the building, where she had been separated from her life. She recalled the cross and sign, *Global Corps./Timeline*. Timeline? What is that? She wondered. Time moves, she thought, and a line is one direction that time can go, like the letter I, or the number 1, into infinity. Also time could move like the waves of the sea, or like the letter O, she intuited, making the sound and shape of an O, which was the ocean. Two Os made an 8, a knot, her father. Half an 8 made an *S*, a river. She pictured *S*-shaped time. Wearily she drifted along the *S*. Exhausted she lay down on the bench and fell to sleep.

— ∞ O ∞ —

A red cat woke Lutz Junior up, meowing. The bench was gone; Lutz Junior found herself under an iridescent metal archway on a paved hill. She knelt down to pet the cat and the cat walked off. Lutz Junior followed her. It began to rain but she took no notice. The cars and buildings were unlike any she had seen before. She heard a piano tinkling and walked towards the sound. The scarves of dusk ebbed away. She followed the dim music until she was under the spiraling lights of a café, The Swan. The sinuous, neon blue *S* mimicked the shape of a swan. Lutz Junior looked through the edge of the café window and saw hands wandering slowly across the keys of an old upright.

— ∞ O ∞ —

Sorrel, at the one-hundred-year-old upright, palpated the notes distractedly. A cold gust blew in. Although she wore a thermal coat and socks, Sorrel was instantly cold. She looked to see who was leaving the door open so inconsiderately. She saw a strange little girl in clumsy, old-fashioned clothing standing in the doorway oblivious to the wind and rain. She had heavy blue trenches under her eyes. Sorrel felt an instinctive sympathy for the girl whose eyes looked so much older than her body. She wasn't dressed for the weather or even the century. Sorrel gently asked the child to come in and close the door. Lutz Junior found a dark corner to sit in and made herself invisible. She looked around in wonder at the unfamiliar objects and strangely dressed people.

The old piano's pedals didn't work very well and some of the keys stuck, but the few people in the room seemed to appreciate Sorrel's song. They tapped their feet and snapped their fingers. Lutz Junior listened. She had never heard anything like it. When Sorrel completed her set she went to the bar and began to drink.

The room was filled with the remnants of a group of revelers who had come to The Swan earlier for a sex-party fashion show. In small rooms, people dressed as authorities had punished people dressed as children. Now everyone who remained assembled around a small wooden stage where Moira, one of the models, was telling jokes that required few words. The crowd laughed whenever she opened her mouth, sometimes even before. Lutz Junior found the woman on stage familiar, though she barely recognized her own tongue in the dialect spoken here.

Sorrel watched Moira move through the crowd once her bit was done and admired the woman's strong body. Greeting friends and strangers, Moira seemed to send out pleasure in all directions. Suddenly she was looking directly at Sorrel, who raised her glass by way of invitation.

— ∞ O ∞ —

Later that night, Sorrel and Moira left together, groping and stumbling along, neither of them noticing the little girl following them home. The moon was full, giving them just enough light to see the rain. Shadows slid around them. Inside, Moira stripped, but Sorrel did not take off her clothes, except for her belt, which she used on Moira, both the leather and the buckle.

Then they drank. Moira told Sorrel stories. She had not always been a comedienne, she said. She had once been a famous artist, before the end of fame. Re-creating canonical performances had been her métier. Sorrel didn't need to ask because she didn't need to be told that Moira was a Transformer. "Transformers invented a new kind of art," Moira said. "It was being forgotten, going extinct. I shot myself with a twentieth century gun in an early performance, impaled myself on a pyramid, sat passively while audiences cut my clothes off with scissors." She described a few of her shows and the effect these shows had on those who witnessed. A single person might appear contemplative, distant, and regard her with the respect granted to a painting. But groups would become shrill, hysterical, and even violent as though, under collective cover, crimes became ceremonies. "Guilt dissolves when everyone participates; the individual burden becomes unnoticeably small," Moira said. She searched for ways to enact her vulnerable performances, but also protect herself. She lay under the floorboards of a gallery and masturbated. People spit on her. She covered her body in shit and blood trying to preempt the audience; she lay with animal corpses on a small platform hung from the ceiling, playing with them as if dolls. One rainy day they prodded her with umbrellas, sitting on each other's shoulders if necessary to reach her. Moira toured widely and rarely encountered an audience that would not devolve in the face of her performances of abjection.

In homage to her forbears, Moira once put a scroll inscribed with political denunciations in her vagina and pulled it out and read it. She tied herself to her lover for a year. Thousands of viewers fired at her with remote-controlled paint-pellet guns. She choreographed public rituals for hundreds of people, which took place under broken freeways, in archaic forts, at abandoned shopping malls. She shared a cage with rats, and traveled to museums in the cage; she mummified herself; she was scarred, pierced, and burned in public. She chanted, shouted, danced, flew, and deployed all manner of apparatuses to recuperate the art of her brief lineage. The number of those who, upon seeing these works, developed the power to change grew smaller and smaller.

"I've never heard of any of that," Sorrel said.

"That's no surprise," Moira replied. Her small, delicate foot was resting on Sorrel's chair between her thighs. Sorrel glanced down and was jarred by the sensation that she was looking at her own disembodied foot. She suppressed a sudden desire to twist Moira's leg in its socket. Images from Moira's stories merged in her mind with dismembered body parts of animals and humans. She related Moira's performances to vivisection. How were all these experiments connected? "Was that considered work, play? Something else?" Sorrel asked. "Art is work," Moira replied. "Trying to make sense, as in sensation, meaning, order. Suffering needs to be represented." "Do you think your art did good?" Sorrel asked. "Art is art," Moira said. "Virtue is good." "Virtue," Sorrel repeated. "I don't think I've ever heard anyone say that word out loud."

— ∞ O ∞ —

Sorrel was up early. She went to let out the cat.

To her astonishment the girl she'd seen at The Swan the night before was on their stairs folded into a ball with her head in her arms, sleeping.

Sorrel sat down next to her. The girl didn't move. Sorrel gently tapped her arm, saying hello, but she didn't stir. Sorrel looked around. The forest across the street was soaked, luminous from the rain. Was there someone moving there in the branches, or was it the light? She squinted.

A muscular cloud swallowed the rising sun. It made a shadow like an open mouth. Sorrel traced the shadow with her finger. She perceived another subtle movement in the trees.

It occurred to her that they were being watched. Was she imagining it? But what's the difference between imagining and knowing? She yawned and thought of coffee. She took a small notebook out of her back pocket, and a pencil. She drew an outline of herself and her shadow, and a cloud and its shadow above her. She imagined they were being shadowed and she thought of that shadow as being knowing.

Lutz Junior opened her eyes and watched Sorrel draw. A moment later Sorrel sensed her gaze and turned her head: their eyes met. Sorrel said hello again. She asked the child if she was OK; where was her mother; was she lost; what was her name? Lutz Junior didn't understand. They sat in silence until Sorrel offered Lutz Junior her notebook and her pencil. Lutz Junior took the pad out of Sorrel's hands. She drew quickly with a sure hand. Eventually she handed the notebook back, put her head back on her knees, and closed her eyes. Sorrel was amazed by the drawing. She didn't recognize the archaic architecture, drawn so realistically it could have been a photograph. But she thought she recalled seeing the enormous white cross the girl had drawn behind the building, with the antique box-store sign on its side next to it, in the old biotext district. She hadn't been in that neighborhood since she was a child. She used to bike around there with her friends. "I know the area," she said. "Do you live around there?" Lutz Junior didn't reply. She willed the young woman to put her hand firmly on her back and moments later she did. Suddenly Lutz Junior began to feel calm. The woman's hand was warm and strong.

Lutz Junior desperately wanted to see her mother, but she also remembered that she had broken her rule already, the night before on the bench. And yet, she reasoned, she had spent the night outside on her own, so perhaps she was no longer bound by her mother's prohibition?

Sorrel would show Lutz Junior the way back to the drawn place. She checked on Moira who was still asleep. Sorrel walked Lutz Junior down a hill and across a deserted thoroughfare. They went several long blocks. Sorrel bought her an apple and put Lutz Junior on an empty trolley, instructing the vessel where to let the child out. The conductor-machine worked the pneumatic pumps and the trolley swiftly rolled along its tracks.

Lutz Junior watched Sorrel's diminishing form as the trolley moved away. The girl had not been in a moving vehicle before, only lived in a static one. She stood on the seats to look out of the window. She leapt from bench to bench easily, and ran up the aisle of the trolley, her weight forward of her body, almost floating. The trolley passed a view of the sea, sparkling like rhinestones. Shortly after they stopped. She got out; she knew the rest of the way. She recalled Sorrel—whorled spikes of reddish-green flowers—and was unafraid. She ate her apple as she walked.

— ∞ O ∞ —

Sorrel went back inside of her apartment. Moira was sitting at the kitchen table. She raised her eyebrows when Sorrel came in. "Sorry," Sorrel explained, "but there was someone outside; she was lost, a child, on my stoop; I was helping her get where she was going, or trying to go, this place—do you know it?" Tearing it out of her notebook she set Lutz Junior's detailed drawing on the table, saying, "I think she was a Transformer at that—look at it." Moira stared at the image and grew very still. "What is this?" she asked cautiously. Sorrel explained again, the girl outside had been trying to get back there. Moira asked, "But how would *you* know it was there?" She stood up and Sorrel realized the woman was looking at her with fear. Not waiting for an answer Moira picked up her things and walked out the door, taking the drawing with her. Bewildered, Sorrel followed. But Moira ran so quickly that she didn't even try to chase her.

Later that day it came to Sorrel that the lot where those old signs were had always been empty. There had never been a building there despite what the girl had drawn. She had imagined it.

— ∞ O ∞ —

Lutz Junior arrived at the rear of the laboratory. Behind the road she marked a dirt path that led to the ocean. She walked around and came to the front entrance. Hare popped out.

Lutz Junior remembered the last time she had seen him, pushing Amber Rose through the little door. "You must be looking for your mother," he said. "No," she said, "I am looking for you." He felt a chill in his motile cells. She was glassing him in. His skin became transparent; his arteries made a lacy filigree. She caused the glass anatomical man to float upwards and hang still in the air. She looked wanting to know: what is he? But it was not possible to tell with her eyes. She closed them and heard ribbons of sound overhead, voices from the roof. She climbed until she was standing on the edge of a blue glass firmament. She gingerly crept on her stomach. She could feel precisely how much weight the sky could take without cracking. She discovered her own weightlessness and, when the chimes seemed to stream up from directly below, carefully looked down.

She saw a family at a table in a small cell. There was nothing in the room but the table, the crockery, the cutlery, and the people, sitting on small wooden benches. A little girl was looking at an empty bowl; across from her were a mother and father. To the side was a toddler in a high chair. A long, heavy piece of metal was taped like a splint to the baby's thumb. She went to suck her thumb. She hit herself on the face with the metal splint and started to cry. The child looked at the baby in the high chair. She appeared to be asking her parents the same question over and over. The parents gave no response, but kept talking to one another as if the girl had not spoken.

Lutz Junior crawled a little further along on her belly to look down into another scene. Several people boarded a bus with a small boy. They sat down and began talking. The little boy picked up a scrap of paper from the empty seat next to him. One of the women turned around and shoved him so that he fell down off his seat onto the floor of the bus. She took the paper from him and yelled at him. The other adults shook their head in disgust at the child, who cried angrily and looked away in shame. Didn't he know any better? they asked him rhetorically. He's such a trial, they complained, such a difficult, difficult trial.

Lutz Junior crawled on. There were twenty-six people in a small crowded courtyard, many naked adults, teenagers, and children running all over, as well as animal babies, old people, and old animals, laying or sitting in corners observing, or tending to some intimate chore. As she watched she slowly understood that each person's individual movement was picked up on and repeated by the person nearest them, and so on down the line so that one could predict, from observing person A, what the activity of person B would next be, and from person Y, the action of person Z, in a cascading order of gestures and actions like an endless ripple that never faded.

Lutz Junior sidled along. A warm orange glow lit up a classroom. Students, their heads bobbing, wore electric masks. If their muscles betrayed the wrong response, if they discoursed inadequately, they received a facial shock. They shook hands with the teacher one by one as they walked in circles talking. Lutz Junior splayed out completely over the glass and used the tips of her fingers and toes to crawl like a spider. She saw people buying and selling other people. She saw prisoners hanging in cells. She saw raped children with their hands on guns, militarized borders, walled-off wealth. She saw rats in mazes, monkeys, rabbits, cats, chickens, and dogs in cages. She saw them being burned, cut, injected, sprayed, dismembered, bludgeoned, gutted, flayed, fed poison, electrocuted, slapped, punched, kicked, pushed, probed, poked, shaved, pumped, exploded, starved, stuffed, laughed at, and ignored. She was sick. She vomited on the flat screen of the world, blurring its surface with her bile. She pushed off the perimeter of the O into the void.

When she looked down again she suddenly saw Amber Rose sitting on a lawn chair, her head lolling to the side, her forefinger hooked in the small glass handle of an empty wine jug, all the windows of their blue van broken. Lutz Junior stared, memorizing her.

As if Lutz Junior's eyes upon her made a sound, Amber Rose woke and looked around perplexed. She looked down at her body. The spaces between her cells had pixilated. Her legs disappeared. She looked up terrified and saw the face of her child looking down at her. She held out her arms—she was dissolving. Lutz Junior reached back, but it was too late. She crawled down as fast as she could. Everything vanished behind her. She leapt the last three feet, but did not feel or hear a sound as she hit the ground, though she knew she had landed.

ACKNOWLEDGMENTS

Another version of "The Coffee Jockey" appeared in "Fantastic Women," *Tin House 33*; thanks to *Tin House* editor Rob Spillman and that issue's guest editor, Rick Moody. Segments of "Transformer" were published as a serial in *Paul Revere's Horse*; thanks to *PRH*'s founding editor Chris Lura. The quote in "Transformer," "Prodigious motion felt and rueful throes … all my nether shape thus grew Transformed," is from *Paradise Lost* by John Milton. My dearest gratitude to Eirik Steinhoff and Thalia Field, as well as Sidebrow editors Jason Snyder, John Cleary, and Kristine Leja for editorial insight and kind encouragement.

Miranda Mellis is the author of *The Spokes* (Solid Objects), *Materialisms* (Portable Press at Yo-Yo Labs), and *The Revisionist* (Calamari Press). She lives and works in San Francisco.

SIDEBROW BOOKS | www.sidebrow.net

SIDEBROW 01 ANTHOLOGY
*A multi-threaded, collaborative narrative, featuring work by
65 writers of innovative poetry and prose*
SB001 | ISBN: 0-9814975-0-0 | DECEMBER 2008

ON WONDERLAND & WASTE
Sandy Florian
Collages by Alexis Anne Mackenzie
SB002 | ISBN: 0-9814975-1-9 | APRIL 2010

SELENOGRAPHY
Joshua Marie Wilkinson
Polaroids by Tim Rutili
SB003 | ISBN: 0-9814975-2-7 | APRIL 2010

CITY
*Featuring work from The City Project by Tyler Flynn Dorholt,
Danielle Dutton, Matt Hart, and Shane Michalik*
SB004 | ISBN: 0-9814975-3-5 | DECEMBER 2010

WHITE HORSE
*A collaborative narrative culled from the White Horse project
and beyond, featuring poetry and prose by 25 writers*
SB006 | ISBN: 0-9814975-5-1 | MARCH 2012

LETTERS TO KELLY CLARKSON
Julia Bloch
SB007 | ISBN: 0-9814975-6-X | MAY 2012

To order, and to view information on new and forthcoming titles,
visit www.sidebrow.net/books.